GEMMA
AND SISTERS

GEMMA AND SISTERS

❧ Noel Streatfeild

A YEARLING BOOK

Published by
Dell Publishing Co., Inc.
1 Dag Hammarskjold Plaza
New York, New York 10017

This work was first published in Great Britain by
William Collins Sons and Co. Ltd.

Yearling ® TM 913705, Dell Publishing Co., Inc.

ISBN: 0-440-42862-9

Printed in the United States of America

First U.S.A. Printing

January 1987

10 9 8 7 6 5 4 3 2

CW

Contents

1 ❧ Gemma

GEMMA LAY IN BED daydreaming. Daydreaming while lying in bed was something that very seldom happened in the last house on the left in Trelawny Drive, Headstone, where the Robinson cousins lived. It wouldn't be happening if Gemma had not been so overexcited by last night's success that she had woken up so early that everybody in the house, including her cousin Ann, whose room she shared, was asleep.

But such a lot has happened to me, Gemma thought. *It's no wonder I can't sleep.* She looked across at the hump in the next bed which was Ann. *A lot has happened to her, too, but although she sings gorgeously, she hasn't got an artistic temperament like I have.*

Gemma sat up in bed and, gripping her knees with her arms, thought back over the past two years. Was it really more than two years ago that she had come to Headstone cross, miserable, and determined to loathe everything? *Goodness, how the cousins must have hated me!* she thought. She saw again in her mind's eye her arrival at the railway station. *How I planned that!* she thought. *Me in my yellow that Mommy and I bought at that new boutique getting out of a first-class carriage!* She flushed as she remembered; then she shrugged her shoulders. *I suppose I was showing off, but who wouldn't? After all, I had been a film star, and who would like*

1

to be pushed off to a place like Headstone? How odd that I hated this house when I first saw it. Mommy had said it would look like that street they used in shots of the orphanage in that film I starred in, and it did then, but not any longer. I love this house now. Well, it's home.

Then Gemma remembered going to school, and even in memory she shuddered. To be sent to a consolidated school had seemed the final horror. She, Gemma Bow, film star, daughter of Rowena Alston, TV and film star, to be stared at as a washed-up failure! It had been Aunt Alice who had thought of changing her name to their name, Robinson. It had been a marvelous idea, and it had sort of worked; only, though she had not wanted anyone to know she was Gemma Bow, she had not wanted to be nobody at all, which is what she was as Gemma Robinson. Gemma smiled to think of herself two years ago. What a silly little thing she had been, making the class behave badly so that she could be important as their leader. But she had been smart, too. It had been a wonderful idea sitting in the headmaster's punishment chair. How she had dared she didn't know. That great black chair outside Mr. Stevens's office, even big boys were scared of being sent to sit in it. But she was glad now she had done it because it got her into the school drama society, and that had got her the leading part in the school pageant, and that in a way had led to last night's triumph.

Funny how things turned out. It was Uncle Philip's mother, whom the cousins called Gran, being jealous that had started everything off. Gran hadn't been able to bear seeing her being a success in the pageant while the cousins had hardly anything to do, so she had suggested they make a group. What a smart idea it had turned out to be! Lydia danced like an angel, so she'd have been a success anyway, but Ann, though she sang divinely, wasn't any good at putting herself over on her own. That was how they all appeared as Gemma and Sisters. It was a good idea letting Robin accompany his own original, as he called it, version of "Oh, Dear, What Can the Matter Be?" Robin was small for eight, so people liked seeing him play the piano, though of course, when proper

2

playing was wanted, Uncle Philip had played, and everybody liked that, too, because they knew, until his hands got stiff, he had been a first violin with the Steen, the town's world-famous orchestra.

Now what next? Of course, Aunt Alice was right when she had said last night that whatever happened to them in the future, Gemma and Sisters would be part of it. But they could not be professionals for a year and six months, for Lydia had been ten last April and it was now only October. It was a silly law, Gemma decided, that would not allow children to have licenses to appear live until they were twelve. *Just look at me*, she thought. *I was working in advertising on TV when I was four and in my first film when I was five, and I wouldn't have fussed if I had an audience looking at me.*

There were signs in the next bed that Ann was waking up. Presently she sat up. Even waking up, Ann was neat, for the night before she had put her straight fair hair into two braids.

"Hello!" Ann looked anxious. "Is it late?"

"Don't flap," said Gemma. "It's Saturday, remember."

Ann got out of bed and put on her dressing gown. "Of course, yesterday was Friday. I had an awful feeling for a moment it was Sunday and I'd be late for choir."

Gemma looked at her silver chiming clock, which she had brought with her when she came to live with the cousins. "You won't be late for anything. It isn't eight o'clock."

"Oh, good!" Ann pulled on her bedroom slippers. "I'll have my bath and then go down and get breakfast. I bet Mom's tired after the concert."

There were some things about the cousins Gemma never would understand. When she had been in pictures, it was taken for granted that if anyone was tired and needed looking after, it was the person who was working. But the cousins didn't understand that. The day after Ann sang in a concert was just like any other day; nobody brought her breakfast up to her in bed or anything like that. If it came to that, nobody had fussed over Cousin Gemma when she had played lead in the school pageant; except at school, they had fussed over her a bit there. Now here was Ann saying Aunt

3

Alice must be tired; actually she was the only person in the house who had had nothing to do last night but watch. However, she let it go, for experience had taught her Ann wouldn't understand and would think she was being mean to Aunt Alice, as she never would be.

Feeling rather grumpy because she had been longing to talk over last night's success with somebody, Gemma lay back on her pillows. She had brought several photographs of her mother with her when she had come to live in the house, but gradually, as the cousins became family, she had packed them away, and when her mother wrote to say she had signed a five-year contract, she had put them all away except one small one. Still, she sometimes in moments of stress spoke to the photograph, for even though she seemed to have thrown her out like an old shoe, Mommy was the one person who could understand about things to do with the theater. Now she rolled over to face the photograph, which was on her half of the chest of drawers.

"Ann makes things so dull, Mommy. Fancy getting up early to get breakfast after a success like last night! That man who came around after the show was Barry Thomas—well, you know all about him. He handles only top people, and he said we were good and . . ." She was going on, but at that moment the door opened, and Lydia, her fair, wavy hair standing on end, looked in.

"Oh, you are awake. Good." She took a flying leap from the door and landed on the end of Gemma's bed. "Where's Ann?"

"Having a bath. She's going down to get breakfast."

"She would!" said Lydia. "She's so good she couldn't be gooder. She always was. Tell me about that man, Gemma. Barry something."

Gemma sat up again. "He handles groups. I mean if he takes us on when you're twelve, we might get anywhere: make records, appear at all the top places. Of course, he'd change us a lot— clothes, production, everything."

"I don't see why he'd change the production," said Lydia. "I thought you produced us smashingly."

Gemma was delighted that Lydia felt she produced well, for that is what she felt herself; still, facts were facts.

4

"There's a lot more to it when you get into the big money."

Gemma was again hugging her knees. Lydia gave them a tap. "It's not Mr. Barry Something we've got to worry about now; it's Ann. She's quite happy singing alone at those concerts she does, and she doesn't mind a bit about production; she thinks as long as she sings all right, it's all that matters. I've been thinking, Gemma, somehow we've got to make the people who have those concerts at Christmas that Ann sings at have all of us."

Where things to do with entertainment were concerned, Gemma was very knowledgeable.

"It's more you I worry about. You are going to be a real dancer. Presently you won't want to be part of a group, and anyway, Miss Arrowhead wouldn't let you."

Miss Arrowhead was Lydia's dancing teacher, who, except on very special occasions, refused to let her pupils dance in public. But Lydia dismissed her with a gesture.

"Don't fuss about her. She won't know. Don't tell anyone, but she didn't know last night. Why would she think I was anything to do with Gemma and Sisters?"

"It's you I'm thinking about. Later on you won't want to be a dancer in a group," Gemma explained. "You'll have to join a ballet, Lydie."

"That's ages away, and when I do, you can get a new me. You don't really need somebody as good as I'm going to be in a group."

Not for the first time Gemma was silenced by Lydia. Extraordinary when you were only ten to be so sure of yourself. Even odder, Lydia, who knew nothing about the professional stage, was right: Someday it would be possible to have another dancer instead of her; she couldn't be the only dancer who could sing a bit.

"As you say, Lydie, that's ages away, and the most important thing now is to get some more concerts, and the best way to do that is through Ann. All those people she sings for at Christmas must see how much nicer it would be to have all three of us instead of just her; they absolutely must."

5

2 ❧ Ann

THE CONCERT at which Gemma and Sisters had made their first appearance had been put on by a committee of which Alice was vice-chair; it worked on behalf of the Headstone hospital. Like the school pageant in which Gemma had acted the leading child, it was part of an all-around effort by Headstone to raise 10,000 pounds to buy kidney machines for the hospital. The 10,000 pounds had actually been raised two weeks before the hospital concert, and there had been a ceremony at the Town Hall to celebrate the fact, so there was not as much excitement about the money raising as there had been. As a result, only a cub reporter had been sent to write up the concert for the Headstone paper, and he was allotted just a small space on a back page, so only those who were at the concert knew what a success the girls had been. Gemma was furious.

"It's sickening, Ann," she grumbled as they walked home from school. "I thought everybody would have heard about us, but nobody had."

"Some were there, I expect," said Ann. "Anyway, what's it matter? Mom was pleased, and that was who we did it for."

As Lydia had remarked, Ann was so good she couldn't be gooder. Gemma wished—not for the first time—that she was a little less good. Surely even a person like Ann could see how

6

glorious it would have been if the whole school had seethed with the news of what a success they had made. However, she bit back what she felt, for it was important to keep Ann in a good mood, and with her mind on the future. She said in what she hoped was a casual way: "I suppose we ought to start rehearsing again. I mean it's not long to Christmas."

Ann was surprised.

"Do you think we'll be asked to give a show at Christmas?"

Gemma could have shaken her, but she kept her head. "Well, you know what Aunt Alice said last night. She said that whatever happened next, she was sure Gemma and Sisters would be part of it."

Ann nodded. "I heard that, but we all were excited last night. I do truly think we needn't rehearse till somebody asks us to give a show, we are all so busy in term time as it is."

Wisely Gemma said no more, but inside she was seething. Oh, dear, how dull Ann was! Luckily there was Lydia to help. Lydia would work like a slave if there were a chance of dancing in public without Miss Arrowhead's knowing.

Ann brooded on that conversation with Gemma. She had long ago accepted that she and Gemma, although they were good friends, as people could not be more unalike. She liked a quiet life, which Gemma detested. Gemma couldn't be happy unless something was going on. Sometimes Ann thought Gemma would rather be in the middle of a row or even a tragedy than that nothing should be happening.

Ann had spoken the truth when she had said they were all so busy in term time it was hard to fit in extra things such as rehearsals. The pupils at the consolidated school were divided into three streams according to the ability of the children. Someone at some time had decided it was kinder to the most backward if they did not know they were in the bottom stream. Of course, those who were in the bottom stream, including Gemma, knew perfectly well where they were whatever their class was called, but it was a rule that A, B, and C must never be used. That term both Ann and Gemma had moved up to the third class. Miss Smith, who was in

7

charge, called her three streams after her dog Meg, so Ann was in 3M and Gemma in 3G. In 3M Ann had to work really hard to keep somewhere near the top of the class. This meant working every minute she was allowed to at her homework, often getting up early to finish what Alice had not permitted her to work at the night before. Sometimes she felt envious of Gemma, who seemed to have settled for the bottom stream, where the work was so much easier she could keep up with no trouble at all.

Then her singing took up a lot of time. Ann was in the school choir, which in the ordinary way practiced one evening a week, but with Christmas coming there would be carols to rehearse, and that would mean an extra evening. Then she was in her church choir; that meant not only choir practices but a busy Sunday. On top of everything else they all were expected to give some help in the house. Every day Ann had to get tea for her mother, who was not back from her part-time work in the hospital. They all had to keep their rooms tidy and take turns to lay the table and wash up. The arrangement about the bedroom was that she tidied it one day, and Gemma the other, but Gemma's idea of tidying was not Ann's, so she found herself tidying after her, for she hated dust and things out of place.

Always when Ann was worried about anything, she turned to her father. Philip Robinson was a really musical man who had loved his work with the Steen orchestra. Though he had put a brave face on it, his heart had nearly broken when a form of rheumatism in his hands had put an end to his career as a violinist. It had been particularly hard to take, for the present leader of the fiddles was getting old, and when he retired, he was to have taken his place. To find himself instead a supernumerary working in the orchestra music library, which was his first job, had been a wretched period to endure. That job had come to an end when he had faced the fact that his hands would never recover sufficiently for him to play the violin professionally, so he had taken up teaching. He worked both privately and for Headstone's big and important music school; he took only really talented pupils and found to his amazement that he was enjoying his new way of life.

8

It was natural there should be a particular affinity between Philip and Ann based on music. Together they planned what she should sing at concerts, and once he had faced the fact that his days with the Steen were over, and therefore there was no point in resting his hands, he became her accompanist. Both he and Ann had bicycles, and when possible, they had bicycled to the concerts, Ann changing after she arrived. But last Christmas the Steen had given a dinner for Philip at which the orchestra and town had made him a presentation. It was a car. Since then he had driven Ann to concerts and sometimes to choir practices. A car is a wonderful place to talk in; on their drives together Philip got to know a lot about his eldest daughter. So when Ann caught him alone and whispered, "Would you drive me to choir practice tomorrow?" he had said, "Yes," certain that Ann had a problem she wanted to discuss.

Sure enough, the next night, as soon as she was in the car, Ann poured out her worries.

"It isn't that doing Gemma and Sisters for Mom's concert wasn't fun," she explained. "It was, but you know what Gemma is when she gets steamed up about anything: She wants more and more of it. I think she and Lydie are hoping people will want Gemma and Sisters at concerts this Christmas instead of just me."

"And you wouldn't like that?" Philip asked.

"Not really, Dad. You see, it will mean a lot of rehearsals, and I'm so busy already."

"But you've always worked very hard at your solos for concerts. Would this be so different?"

Ann gave a deep sigh. "You've not worked with Gemma. It's all the little things which I don't think matter. How we come on the stage. How we stand when somebody else is doing something and, worst of all, bows. You wouldn't believe how Gemma fusses about bowing; we've all got to do it exactly alike and at the same moment. You see, she made what are called personal appearances when she had a new film, so she's used to it. But when I'm singing at a concert by myself, I never bother to think how I bow or how I come on and off the platform, I just do it, and that's that."

9

In the dark of the car Philip smiled. It was true. Ann's exits and entrances, if he had to be honest, had always been awkward. He thought a course of training by Gemma would do Ann a lot of good. However, he was not going to tell her that outright. Besides, there was another point of view which he could show her.

"I'm sorry you feel like that about Gemma and Sisters, though I see what you mean. It's selfish of me, but I, too, hoped there would be lots more performances. You know, when you've performed in public for as long as I did, you miss it, and you miss the talk behind the scenes. The evening of Mom's concert I enjoyed more than I had enjoyed anything for ages. Particularly it was fun chewing it all over afterward, eating supper."

Ann thought about this. Then she said: "There's another thing, Dad: The songs I sing are good music; do you think they sound right mixed up with Robin's stuff and 'There Was a Lady Loved a Swine' that Gemma sings to her banjo and tap dancing?"

Philip considered that. "I think it's all right. Good music is always good music and I've never heard you sing better than you did at Mom's concert."

They were at the church. Ann stayed for a moment before she got out of the car. "I'm a bit surprised at your feeling like that, but I expect you're right, and I do understand about you. What will you do when people ask me to sing at a concert? Will you tell them about Gemma and Sisters or what?"

Philip gave her a kiss. "Run along or you'll be late, and don't sound so anxious. The news about Gemma and Sisters will get around, you'll see."

10

3 ❧ Lydia

LYDIA WAS HAVING three private dancing lessons from Miss Arrowhead each week, and she joined her general class on Saturdays as well. This was made possible because of Lydia's own efforts. When Philip first learned he had something the matter with his hands, he had decreed that for the time being none of his children could take extras because until his future was decided, he could not afford it. Lydia had refused to accept that she must give up her dancing classes, so without her mother or Polly, Miss Arrowhead's niece who was teaching her, knowing anything about it, she had slipped into one of Miss Arrowhead's classes and had persuaded her to watch her dance. The result was that she was taught for nothing.

One opportunity to dance before an audience had gone to Lydia's head like wine. It took all the willpower she had not to boast to the other girls in the Saturday class about what a success she had been, but fear kept her silent. It would be too awful to think about if Miss Arrowhead found out.

Miss Arrowhead was not easy to fool, so the very first lesson after the concert at which Gemma and Sisters had made their first appearance, she spotted something different in Lydia's work. Even her pliés were performed as if an audience were watching her. Polly lived with Miss Arrowhead, and usually in the evening they discussed what had happened during the day.

"I don't know whether to tackle Lydia or not," Miss Arrowhead told Polly. "That time when she slipped a fast one over you and crept into my class to demand that I see her dance, I told her, you remember, because she had told a lie to get an interview with me, I couldn't trust her, and she said—and these are her exact words— 'I'll never tell you a lie as long as I live. I absolutely promise I won't.'"

Polly laughed. "I'm sure she meant it at the time. I can just hear her saying it."

Miss Arrowhead nodded. "So far there has been no opportunity for her to lie, but I wonder what evasive tactics we should see if I ask her point-blank if she had danced without permission."

"And if she says yes?" Polly said.

Miss Arrowhead gave Polly a look. "There's the rub. I simply cannot let Lydie go. Imagine in a long life of teaching if I really have found a winner! That is something which happens to very few dancing teachers."

"Then if I were you," Polly suggested, "I wouldn't say anything. If somehow you find out, I suppose you'll have to tell her off, but otherwise I wouldn't know anything about it. Is she dancing badly?"

"That's what's so maddening. Her dancing is, if anything, improved. She seems to me to be trying harder; it is as if she had something to work for now."

Polly laughed. "You know I don't agree with your rule about the children dancing in public. A dancer's training is very hard, so an occasional public performance might be a help."

"But so unsettling. The children taking part must be carefully rehearsed; that would mean they would have to be taken off their usual routine for weeks."

Polly nodded. "I see that, but I still believe in a stimulus."

Miss Arrowhead gave a deep sigh. "There's stimulus enough coming for Lydie if she continues to improve. She can't of course go to that consolidated school while training for the ballet; something else must be arranged for her. She'll be eleven in April."

"That means if she goes to the consolidated, it will be this time next year."

12

"That's right, and somehow I've got to find an alternative. She would never manage her classes with me plus all the homework she would have to do."

"Would the right answer for her be the Royal Ballet School if she could get a place?" Polly asked. "But of course, you'd hate that. Why should you let her go?"

Miss Arrowhead laughed. "You must think you've got an incredibly selfish aunt. I would love Lydie to get into the Royal Ballet School if she could, but the competition is fierce, and even if she was accepted, I don't see her family allowing her to go. They are very united, and I think they would say no."

"Oh, well," said Polly, "perhaps we'll have a bright idea by next year or that Mr. Stevens, who is headmaster, may see a way to cut down Lydie's homework. In the meantime, let's keep our thumbs crossed that if Lydie has been breaking your rule and dancing in public, nobody tells you about it. Then you'll never need to take any action."

But somebody did tell Miss Arrowhead about Gemma and Sisters, and a very jealous somebody. In the Saturday dancing class Lydia worked with a girl called Rosie Glesse. Since she had been able to toddle, Rosie's mother had known her child was a genius. She had bored every other mom who had a small daughter to death telling them how Rosie could walk on her pointes with only socks on her feet.

When she was five, Rosie had joined Polly's dancing class, and when she was nine, she had moved up into Miss Arrowhead's classes. She became, from Miss Arrowhead's point of view, a conscientious dancer, but that was all. There was no link between Rosie the dancer and Rosie the person. In barre work this was not noticeable, but in center practice she found her a dull child, and when it came to mime, she was hopeless.

"Oh, well," Miss Arrowhead would say to Polly, "I suppose she may get into a troupe someday, but she's a terrible bore to teach."

Unfortunately Rosie's mother did not see Rosie as Miss Arrowhead saw her. To her she was what she frequently called her—"my little Pavlova." Whenever she met Miss Arrowhead, she was full of what teachers at school and people who had met Rosie had said. "The vicar's wife said you had only to look at Rosie to see talent written all over her. The teacher at the school who takes the girls in barefoot dancing says Rosie makes all the other children look like tin soldiers."

Mrs. Glesse generally fetched Rosie from her dancing classes, and always from the one on Saturday mornings, for after it they went shopping. Parents were not allowed in the studio itself, but there were windows through which they could watch what was going on. All too often in Mrs. Glesse's opinion a small fair child was picked out to demonstrate what Miss Arrowhead wanted, a child who was not a patch on her Rosie. She had asked Rosie who the child was, and Rosie had said casually: "Oh, that's Lydie. She's ever so good. Miss Arrowhead gave her a scholarship, so she teaches her for nothing."

Mrs. Glesse did not mind about the free lessons, for her husband was a rich man; that was why Rosie went to a private school, and it did not matter how much was spent on extras like dancing. But she did mind another child's being picked out for notice, and she did mind the calm way Rosie said "ever so good." That was the worst of Rosie; she wouldn't assert herself. So when Mrs. Glesse saw Lydia not only dancing a solo on a stage but bringing the house down with applause, she felt, as she told her sister, who had gone to the concert with her, as sick as she had felt on the boat going to Guernsey.

It had not been possible to make Rosie tell Miss Arrowhead about the concert.

"Oh, Mom, I couldn't. I like Lydie, and Miss Arrowhead will be ever so cross; she might take away Lydie's scholarship."

And a very good thing too, thought Mrs. Glesse, but it wasn't a good idea to say so. Instead, she said: "Oh, well, if you won't, I will. Fair's fair; if that child can dance in public, so can you."

The next Saturday after the class she marched into the studio and faced Miss Arrowhead. "You weren't at the concert for the hospital, were you? But I suppose you knew because you had rehearsed her."

14

Miss Arrowhead shook her head. "What happened?"

"Well, if you had been there, you would have seen Lydia Robinson dancing one solo and a tap dance with one of the other girls. There were three. They call themselves Gemma and Sisters."

"Thank you," said Miss Arrowhead in a dismissing voice. "I didn't rehearse Lydie, so I didn't know. I will have a word with her."

"I should think so," said Mrs. Glesse. "Well, I mean to say, if Lydie can do it, so can others. I'm sure time can be found for rehearsals. I'm worn out saying no to people who want Rosie to dance at concerts."

"Quite." Miss Arrowhead agreed. "As I say, I will talk to Lydie."

At Lydia's next private class Miss Arrowhead said: "Lydie, is it true you danced at a concert run by the hospital?"

Lydia flushed. "Well, actually it wasn't like it sounds. I was part of three; we call ourselves Gemma and Sisters. We did it for Mom; she couldn't get anything new for the concert. I didn't exactly say you had given permission, but she thought you had said I could dance."

"Indeed! And what did you dance?"

"It was difficult to choose," Lydia explained. "You see, we wore black plastic, which is only right for a few things. So I did a sort of doll dance I learned with Polly; it was pretty babyish, so I added to it a bit."

"And that was all?"

Lydia remembered her promise never to tell Miss Arrowhead a lie. "Well, we sang and . . ."

"And what, Lydia?"

"Well, my cousin Gemma learns tap, and she taught me. We did that. Gemma arranged everything; she's awfully good at arranging."

A doll dance and a tap dance to help the hospital sounded very harmless, but rules were rules.

"Well, this once I'll let it pass, but there is to be no more dancing in public. Is that clear?"

Lydia's mouth set tight. Her blue eyes glared at Miss Arrowhead.

15

"No. It's going to happen again. Lots and lots of times. You only said we couldn't dance by ourselves, but I'm not. Ann and Gemma are both on the platform with me. Ann's always singing at concerts, and it doesn't do her any harm. Why should doing a dance hurt me?"

Why should it? It was the thin end of the wedge, and Miss Arrowhead knew it. Every child she taught would want permission to dance in public if she gave way now. But Lydia had made a point: She was part of a group; she was not dancing a solo. Miss Arrowhead looked at the child's angry face and smiled.

"Let us get on with your lesson. I think if I have your promise you will only dance as Gemma and Sisters, I might give you permission, but you must always tell me so that I can rehearse you."

"Good," said Lydia. "I knew you'd see it my way."

4 ⚭ Robin Arranges

IT WAS ROBIN who arranged the next appearance of Gemma and Sisters. His name was not really Robin. He had been christened Sebastian after Bach, of whose music Philip was particularly fond. However, nobody could go through life being called Sebastian—and you can't really shorten it—so instead, he used Robin because it was the first half of his surname. When he was eight, he had been awarded a scholarship for St. Giles Choir School, where he was doing very well indeed, for he had a lovely voice and perfect pitch. In fact, though Robin did not know it, the choirmaster had his eye on him as a future solo boy.

Although Robin was doing so well in the choir school and sang church music very nicely indeed, his heart was given to another side of music. He liked writing it, not original material but what he called "swirling" well-known tunes. He had been enchanted to hear his sisters and Gemma singing his version of "Oh, Dear, What Can the Matter Be?" accompanied by himself on the piano. The only trouble was just doing it once wasn't enough. It was such fun he wanted it to happen often. At the choir school Robin had a redheaded friend called Nigs—short for Nigel—who was a great admirer of his original tunes, so he told him how he felt.

"The concert had been ghastly. Then the girls came on, and you should have seen the way all the old trouts sat up. They started

17

with my swirled 'Oh, Dear, What Can the Matter Be?' and I must say they sang it pretty good."

Nigs had often been to tea at Trelawny Drive, so he knew all the Robinsons.

"I wouldn't have thought that was your sister Ann's sort of music."

"It isn't, but when they were learning the music, Gemma made me teach it them to show how it ought to go—well, it's getting the beat right that matters—you know how it is when a thing's swirled. And anyway, Ann couldn't sing like she does ordinarily because she has much more voice than Gemma or Lydie, so she learned to do it the way I wanted."

"I thought it would go all right," said Nigs. "I always told you it wasn't bad. Are you doing some more?"

Robin groaned. "That's just it. You know what Ann is, always yapping about how she ought to do her homework—she's that sort of girl. So I bet she won't even think about Gemma and Sisters until the Christmas holidays, which is miles away."

"If they do it again," Nigs asked, "will they sing 'Oh, Dear, What Can the Matter Be?' or will you suggest something new for them?"

"That's what I'd like, but I know Ann; she'll say she has no time to rehearse a new one." Robin gave Nigs a nudge. "So what I want is for someone to ask the girls to do their stuff. I have a feeling Mom and Dad might say it was a good idea, and then, if she liked it or not, Ann would have to learn something new; I mean, they can't do the same old stuff each time, can they?"

Nigs had an idea.

"You know my dad is something posh, being a Rotarian. They're always getting money for something. This year, so far, it's all been for the ten thousand pounds for the kidney machines, but now they've got those, I bet he'll be pushing for something else."

The love of Nigs's life was drums. He was planning to be the drummer of a world-famous group when he grew up. Robin, of course, knew this, but he knew, too, how hard it was for Nigs to practice because his mother, an otherwise reasonable person as grown-ups go, was most unreasonable about drum playing in the house, and the neighbors weren't too keen on it either. Now he had an idea.

"If you get your father steamed up to use Gemma and Sisters, I'll swirl a tune that needs drums. Then you'll have to practice, and anyway, there'll be rehearsals at my house."

Nigs thought that a splendid idea. "Don't flap. It's as good as in the bag. You get on with your swirling."

It was Sunday two weeks later that a triumphant Nigs waited before matins for Robin outside St. Giles Church.

"It's in the bag or almost. My dad will talk to your dad."

Together the boys went into the choir vestry to put on their scarlet cassocks.

"How did you do it?" Robin asked.

"Easy. Dad said to Mom that something had to be done about repairs to the old people's home, but that the town had been drained dry of talent earning the ten thousand pounds for the kidney machines. So I said I'd heard that Gemma and Sisters was smashing, and then I had a bit of luck. Mom said wasn't that the Robinson girls and their cousin because somebody who was at the concert had raved about them. Have you swirled a tune with drums in it?"

Robin arranged the pleated frill that the choir wore so that it wouldn't scratch his ears.

"It's almost finished. It's called 'The Little Woman.' It's pretty idiotic, but it's got a good tune. It starts 'There was a little woman, as I've heard say, Fol, lol, did-dle, did-dle dol.' Well, almost every line—and there are lots of them—finishes with the Fol, lol bit, and that needs a drum and—"

The choirmaster had been looking in a meaningful way at Robin and Nigs. He could be very sarcastic. "If it would not inconvenience you two to finish your conversation, I would be grateful if you would take your places ready to move into church."

Nigel's father, whose name was George Gamesome, was the sort of person who got things done. Having said he would ask Philip

19

about Gemma and Sisters for a concert for repairs to the old people's home, he got on with it. He telephoned Philip at the music school and asked him to lunch. When they met, he wasted no time beating about the bush. He had heard, he said, Gemma and Sisters well spoken of; money must be raised to repair the old people's home before it fell down.

"Do you think, Robinson, your kids would do their stuff? This home is something we Rotarians feel very strongly about."

Philip, after the children were in bed, had a talk with Alice. He told her what George Gamesome wanted.

"I haven't said yes, and I haven't said no. The problem is Ann. She's already talked to me about concerts in term time; she says she's too busy—you know, homework, school choir, church choir—all the rest of it."

Alice was mending one of Philip's shirts. For a time she went on with her work while she turned over in her head what he had told her. Then she said: "Ann doesn't get much free time; it's all a question of priorities. I know her schoolwork is desperately important, but so is Ann all over. I sometimes think she is so wrapped up in her books and choir practice that there is no time left for the real Ann to grow."

"So you think another stab at Gemma and Sisters would be a good idea?"

"It might. It certainly took some of the stiffness out of her last time. She wasn't the serious girl we've seen singing solos, and whatever she says now, I have a feeling she enjoyed it. Anyway, there won't be much rehearsing; they know what they've got to do."

Philip smiled. "Don't you believe it. Haven't you heard our son playing his version of the old woman whose skirts were cut up to her knees by a peddler?"

"Oh, is that what that tune is? I suppose he's swirling it."

"That's right." Philip agreed. "And my guess is he intends Gemma and Sisters to sing it."

"Oh, dear, that'll mean rehearsals," said Alice. "Ann won't like that."

Philip got up to make them both a cup of tea.

20

"The concert's not until December, I think Saturday and Sunday rehearsals should be enough."

Alice put down her sewing. "I must say I'm pleased. I nearly burst with pride at the first concert. I don't mind telling you I hope there are a lot more."

Philip nodded. "I'm sure Gemma and, of course, Lydie would agree with you. I'll let Gamesome know tomorrow that he can have Gemma and Sisters."

5 ⚮ Audience Participation

As SOON AS the news broke that there was to be another Gemma and Sisters concert, true to her arrangement, Lydia told Miss Arrowhead what was planned.

"I don't really want to do that doll dance again, but black plastic isn't right for lots of things."

"What are the dresses like?" Miss Arrowhead asked.

Lydia tried to explain. "Well, first there's a top that has buttons down the front and that's got elastic between our legs to keep it down. We wear ordinary very short black pants, and over them we have very mini black pleated skirts. There aren't any sleeves, but we have big white collars we button on which have a bow in front."

"And what shoes?"

"Patent. Gemma's and mine have tips on for our tap dance. Then, when Ann is singing, I change into black dancing shoes like I wear to your lessons. They are waiting on the top of the piano."

While Lydia was describing the dresses Miss Arrowhead, who was sitting at her desk, had been drawing on her blotting paper. "Like this?"

Lydia leaned against Miss Arrowhead's chair while she had a look. "That's very good. It's almost exactly right except our collars aren't as big as that."

"I don't see why," Miss Arrowhead suggested, "if you are going

22

to change your shoes while Ann is singing, you could not make other changes. With a scarf instead of that collar and an apron you could dance your Irish jig."

Lydia was enchanted. "When I learned with Polly, we did an umbrella dance. I could easily do that. The dance was rather feeble, but you could make it much better, and there's dozens of dances that just want caps like that Dutch dance and that Yugoslavia thing."

Miss Arrowhead laughed. "Don't get carried away too far. We can spend only a short while at each lesson on these dances. For the moment I think we'll concentrate on the Irish jig."

Gemma was not at first enthusiastic about Lydia's ideas for further dressing up. "But when Ann's singing, nobody ought to look at anybody but her. If you're fussing around changing into aprons and things, the audience might look at you."

Privately Lydia hoped that was just what the audience would be doing, but of course, she didn't say so.

"I'll change as quiet as a mouse."

Gemma saw the stage in her mind's eye. She saw Ann singing, her lovely voice pouring out over the audience, but she saw, too, the distraction caused by Lydia, who did not know how to keep in the background. Then she had an idea: "I know, we'll both be offstage while Ann sings. I'll work out how we do it so it looks part of the act. Then, when you've done your dance, you can just throw your scarf and apron on the piano and put on your collar in front of the audience. I'll work out how we do everything so as to give you time for that."

With Robin's new swirled nursery rhyme, Lydia's new dance, and a new song for Ann, Gemma and Sisters seemed almost a new show from their first appearance more than a month ago. The only unchanged thing about it was Gemma's own solo. Although she had starred in films since she was five, she had not, when she came to live with the cousins, had a talent suitable for concerts, for she was an actress, and actors, she had explained, needed other actors unless they were great and could recite yards of Shakespeare by themselves. So, not to be out of things, she had decided—advised

23

by her Uncle Philip—to learn the banjo, an instrument she had been taught for one film and had enjoyed learning.

A young man called Ted Smith was engaged to teach Gemma. She had got on quite well and at last had learned to accompany herself in a song. She had not much voice, but a wistful quality, which had endeared her to her film public, came over well, as did her natural charm. But she had only the one song so far, the one she had sung in Gemma and Sisters: "There Was a Lady Loved a Swine."

"Come on, Gemma," Ted would urge. "It's silly sticking always to the same song. I know you need suiting, but there's plenty more you could manage."

Gemma wouldn't learn another. She knew that her ability was slender but that she could put over "There Was a Lady Loved a Swine," and she was scared to venture further. However, the fact that here was the only old material in the second edition of Gemma and Sisters made her wonder if she ought to learn something new. As usual she took her trouble to Philip.

"Uncle Philip, as you know, I was going to sing the same song in Gemma and Sisters, but do you think I ought to learn another? Ted wants me to."

Philip looked at Gemma with understanding. "But you don't feel ready for that yet?"

Gemmna tried to explain. "You see, I'd been working in films so long, somehow I thought I always would. It was awful when the management didn't renew my contract. Oh, they said things like me being too old for children's parts but they'd probably use me again when I was in my teens, but it didn't mean anything. Well, you know how washed up I felt when I first came here."

"And then there was the pageant"—Philip prompted her—"and then Gemma and Sisters, both a success, so you didn't want to run any risk of not being a success."

"Well, not a success exactly," Gemma said. "I know I can't sing like Ann, and I can only just get by on the banjo, but I know now because I've done it that I can put that song over, and I'm scared to try another."

Philip smiled. "I sympathize. If I were you, I would work at two or three more songs, and stick to the lady and her swine for the next concert, but if, as I expect, there are several more, I think you will have to bud out with something new."

Gemma gave him a hug. "I knew you'd understand. I will learn some more. Ted's got some lined up, but when I've learned them, you've got to hear them before they go in the show."

Philip nodded. "That's a bargain."

Although rehearsals could be only on Saturdays and Sundays, Gemma worked every minute of the day that she could spare on Gemma and Sisters, and lots that she could not, so quite soon she was in trouble at school. It came from her form teacher, Miss Smith, but it was the result of complaints from almost everybody who taught Gemma.

"Gemma," said Miss Smith, "stay behind after school. I want a word with you."

Gemma felt as if her insides were going down an elevator. Now that she thought about it, there had been a lot of "Please attend, Gemma." "Gemma, you aren't attending," and from one teacher who was sarcastic: "I teach you for only two periods a week, Gemma. Is it too much to ask for a little of your attention?"

It was strange how large a room 3G looked when all the class except Gemma had left. Miss Smith didn't help, for at first she said nothing. Instead, she corrected books. At last she put down her pen and looked at Gemma. So far Miss Smith had not meant much to her class except that it was known she had a dog called Meg after whom the three divisions of the class were initialed. At a casual glance Miss Smith was a nondescript-looking young woman with mousy hair and rather a sallow complexion, but now that her full attention was fixed on her, Gemma saw what she had not noticed before: that she had beautiful dark eyes. *I wouldn't wonder if she's photogenic*, she thought.

"I find it very wearing," said Miss Smith, "when every time I go into the staff common room, I am greeted on all sides by grumbles about your inattention in class. I am particularly surprised it should be you of whom everyone complains, for you should understand the meaning of audience participation."

Gemma gazed at Miss Smith, puzzled. What was audience participation? Why should she understand it?

"Why me?"

Miss Smith fixed her eyes on Gemma. "You acted—and very well, too—in the school pageant last term. You had to tell the story of Headstone."

There had been two children in the pageant, a boy as well as the girl.

"And Sammy," Gemma reminded Miss Smith.

"You and Sammy," Miss Smith said, "but you had most of the speaking to do. How would you have felt if you had noticed that when you were speaking, the audience was not bothering to attend?"

"I'd have thought them crazy because unless they listened, they wouldn't know what the next scene was about."

"Exactly." Miss Smith agreed. "And when you don't attend, we know you won't know what the next class is about."

"But that's different," Gemma protested. "That was a pageant and fun; you can't compare it with lessons."

"I can and do," said Miss Smith. "You, when you are in class, are the audience, just as when a person is preaching in church, the congregation is the audience. If the audience doesn't participate— that is to say, listens and learns—there might just as well be no teaching or preaching. You can be cheap and say, 'And a good job, too,' but that's nonsense, and you know it.' However, I've not kept you in today to tell you this but to warn you: If there is any more inattention, I am writing to your aunt to ask if someone could supervise your homework, and I am telling her why."

Gemma stared so hard at Miss Smith that she got out of focus; there was only a blur sitting at the desk. If that letter was written, it was good-bye to Gemma and Sisters except in the holidays. At once Aunt Alice would know why she wasn't attending.

"Please don't write to Aunt Alice. I will attend. Truly I will. In fact, now I know about audience participation, I wouldn't wonder if I was the most attentive girl you ever taught."

Miss Smith suppressed a smile. "Very well, Gemma. You can go now. But never let me have to speak to you about inattention again, for if I do, I promise you I shall write that letter. That is a certainty."

6 ᘒ Preparations

IN SPITE OF Miss Smith's threat, Gemma found it terribly difficult to stop her mind from wandering in class. Attending at lessons was always difficult for her, for she had been given a bad start. Because it was impossible for her as a small child to fit in her filmwork with attending ordinary school, her mother had engaged a governess called Miss Court. Miss Court had been quite a good governess, but she had lost her head over Gemma. She thought that she was the most wonderful little actress and that it was a privilege to teach her, and she had often told Gemma this. As a result, Gemma had more or less done what she liked. She had enjoyed English and history, so spent most of lesson time on these subjects. She had detested arithmetic and geography and so was always finding reasons to miss a lesson. Because of this poor start, Gemma had arrived at Headstone Consolidated very backward in important subjects; that was why she had been placed in the lowest stream of class 1, about which she had written sadly to her mother, "You can't sink lower than 1E."

If Gemma had really tried, she could have got out of the bottom stream into the second, but she never had tried. Other ways which helped her not to feel inferior turned up. First there was a silly patch in which she became the class ringleader in behaving badly. Then there was the pageant; that had helped a lot because her performance had been seen by the whole school. She had moved up twice as well. She was still in the lowest stream, but at least now she was in class 3; that was better than being in class 1. She had outside interests as well. She really enjoyed her banjo lessons with Ted. Then there was dancing. She would never be much of a dancer—she was not good enough for Miss Arrowhead to teach—but she enjoyed Polly's classes, especially when there was mime. And there was tap dancing. She went to the Headstone Drama School to learn this. It made her Saturdays one long rush, for first she had her lesson with Polly, then home for her banjo class; then immediately after she had swallowed her lunch, she had to rush off, clutching her tap shoes. Although she had only one tap lesson a week, she had to work at it every evening, for Lydia, who usually came to watch her classes, refused to listen to excuses but nagged at her until she put on her shoes and taught her the new steps she had learned, though often, with Lydia having watched the lesson, it was the other way around, and it was Lydia who had to teach Gemma.

Gemma had to write a letter every Sunday to her mother. It had become rather a chore. It was two years and a half since they had seen each other, and that's a very long time when one lives in Hollywood and the other in Headstone, for there was less and less to write about.

It was easier for her mother, Gemma thought, because she worked at a big studio, making films for TV, and often met actors and actresses they both knew. Then there was the film she was making to write about; Gemma was always interested to hear about that. But it was very different for Gemma; she had written to her mother about the pageant and about Gemma and Sisters, but she guessed she was not really interested, dismissing both as amateur theatricals, which she had always scorned. It was this feeling which made Gemma the following Sunday write about school, a subject she had scarcely mentioned before, knowing it would bore her mother. But now, having no one else she could tell, she poured out her troubles:

29

I know old Courty was a sweetie but I didn't learn much
with her. Headstone Consolidated is enormous so every
class is divided into three, really A, B, and C, but they
aren't called that because there is an idiotic idea that if the
streams aren't called A, B, and C, we shan't know we are in
the lowest stream, which is where I am. Ann and I are in
the same class, but Ann is in the top stream. The trouble
about the lowest stream is that half my stream simply haven't
any brains at all—that's true, I'm not making it up—so all
lessons have to be footling to suit them. Well, as you know,
I'm a dumb cluck when it's arithmetic or geography but not
bad at English and history, and honestly the way they're
taught would be okay for a kid of eight, so of course, I don't
attend—well, who would? Anyway, this week I got blasted
because I wasn't attending—which I wasn't because we're
doing a repeat of Gemma and Sisters and I was planning
entrances and exits for it. I don't think I've ever told you
much about school before, so I thought today I would—it's
not bad for lots of things and Ann likes it awfully; it's just
me that's wrong, I suppose.

There had been nothing in her mother's letters to Gemma to
suggest she had her on her conscience. She had originally gone to
Hollywood to make one film, but the rushes had pleased everybody, and her contract had been renewed for what proved in the
end to be five years. "I am afraid, darling," she had written, "we
may be parted for a long time." Her mother had tried to soften the
news, so she had told Gemma she had instructed her lawyers to
send her 200 pounds so that she could take all the Robinson family
for a holiday; this had happened, and a glorious holiday it was. But
her mother had not said she had sent the money because she felt
she was neglecting her child, which is what sometimes she did feel.
If Gemma had known this, she would not have said what she did
about Headstone Consolidated, or at least she would have worded
her letter differently. But not knowing, she licked up her airmail

30

letter and mailed it without a thought that a day might come when she would give anything to have it back.

The rehearsals for Gemma and Sisters were fun; even Ann enjoyed them. Nigs was a great success on the drums, and all three girls liked Robin's swirled version so much that at any hour someone would be heard singing "There was a lit-tle woman, as I've heard say, Fol, lol, did-dle, did-dle dol."

The Rotarians, having decided to raise money to restore the old people's home, did it in style. They hired a hall called the Winter Garden. This had lots of advantages, including modern stage lighting, good curtains, and a fine variety of backcloths and stage effects. It was Nigs who brought the news. He came to a rehearsal bursting to tell it.

"Dad says it's the Winter Garden. . . ."

He waited for the oohs and aahs to die down, for the Winter Garden was considered by Headstone the classy place in which to hold a concert.

"And Dad says," Nigs went on, "would somebody go and see the stage manager; his name is Mr. Rumage. I said that would be you, Gemma; it's to tell him what you want, like lighting and pianos and things."

"I know Charles Rumage," said Philip. "I'll phone him and make an appointment, and we'll go and see him together, Gemma."

The concert was to be held on the first Saturday in December.

"Not too near Christmas for people to have spent all their money," Mr. Gamesome stated, "but near enough to give a start to the festive season."

"Thank goodness it's a Saturday," Ann said when she heard the date was fixed. "It won't interfere with homework, and the concert will be over before the extra choir practices for carols at church and the school choir start."

"I'll keep myself free around the concert so that I can chauffeur you about," Philip said.

Alice smiled at that. "Hark who's talking. Have you thought who'll be here for the concert? Remember she considers Gemma and Sisters her creation."

31

"My goodness, Gran!" said Lydia. "Of course, she'll want to be here. She'll be thrilled, and she'll say it's a sad heart that never rejoices."

Gran was Philip's mother. She was a widow with five sons and daughters. Though she had a home of her own, she spent most of the year visiting her children. She expected to spend at least six weeks with her son Philip, and this did not include special occasions, such as the pageant last year and the first performance of Gemma and Sisters. It was in fact she who had talked to Gemma about forming a family group. It was not admiration for Gemma but a wish to see her grandchildren shine which had prompted the suggestion. She was proud of Ann, Lydia, and Robin, and it had made her quite ill when she came to see the pageant to find that though Ann sang, it was only with the choir, and Lydia danced as one of a hundred fairies and Robin was not performing at all, while the star of the whole show was her daughter-in-law Alice's niece.

Gran was loved by her grandchildren, though secretly they also thought her a joke because her conversation was packed with proverbs. To Gemma she was a frightening old woman, and though they had come to a sort of truce the last time they had met, it still made Gemma feel cold inside to think that she was again coming to stay.

The truce had happened on the Sunday after the pageant. Gemma was feeling flat anyway, as anybody would who had been living at high pitch for a week and had come down with a bump back to normal life. The cousins and Philip and Alice were out, so Gemma had settled down with a book in the garden. It was there Gran had found her. She had said: "I'm glad to have this talk with you, for I know who you are. You are Gemma Bow, aren't you?"

For so long Gemma had called herself Gemma Robinson that she had begun to feel safe. Nobody knew who she was, they had no idea she had once been the famous Gemma Bow, and nobody was ever going to know. Why, even Gran had thought her surname was Alston, the same as Mommy's. How had she found out the truth? She had tried to hide from Gran how upset she was.

32

"Yes," she had said, "but I don't want anybody to know. That's why Aunt Alice suggested I call myself Robinson."

Gran had sniffed, and out had popped a proverb. "Oh, what a fearful web we weave when once we practice to deceive. But you being Gemma Bow could have its uses. You are accustomed to making a show of yourself in public, anyone can see that." Then Gran had explained what she had in mind. It was what was to turn out to be Gemma and Sisters.

"If the children appear as a group," she said, "it will draw attention to the Robinsons as a family. Mine is a very clever family, and people should know about them."

Gemma was thinking so hard about that talk in the garden on a Sunday in June that for the time being she had left the tea table and the family discussing the concert. Alice was the first to notice this. "What are you dreaming about, Gemma? You were miles away. Was it the concert?"

Gemma pulled herself back from her talk with Gran. "Sort of. I find knowing the date makes it feel very near. I was thinking if old Mrs. Robinson is coming, how important it is that everybody should be good."

7 ❧ Winter Garden Concert

EARLY ON THE morning of the concert day Lydia put her head around Ann and Gemma's bedroom door. "I heard Ann go to her bath, so I came down for company. I feel wormish inside anyway, but it's worse when you're all by yourself."

When Gemma came to live in the house, it was decided she should share the room with Ann and for Lydia a tiny storeroom should be turned into a bedroom. This left the spare room free for visitors such as Gran. Usually Lydia loved her room and was proud of it, but Gemma knew what Lydia meant about wormishness being worse when you were alone.

"It's all right for you, Lydie," she said comfortingly, "you know your dance will go down well, but even though I've done it before, I'm scared to death of 'There Was a Lady Loved a Swine.' "

Lydia pulled the bottom of Gemma's eiderdown around her. "It's not my dance, Gemma; it's those awful songs. It's all right for Ann, but I'm scared I'll sing wrong; I easily could."

It had been decided the girls should start with "There Was an Old Woman as I've Heard Say," and the show should wind up with Robin's swirled version of "Oh, Dear, What Can the Matter Be?" which they had sung at the first concert.

"You can't be more scared than I am," said Gemma, "and your gran being here makes me feel worse, and I'm worried as well that

34

the order doesn't work right. Obviously we must do our step dance first so we can dance off and leave Ann on the stage to sing her song. But suppose we can't hear the music or something, and we don't come back in time for your Irish jig, and you can't think how I wish we weren't finishing with me. It will hang over me all the time."

"Imagine"—Lydia groaned—"all the day to live through before the concert."

Ann had come from her bath in time to hear this. She could see Gemma and Lydia were what she called "working themselves up," so she spoke in a brisk voice. "I wouldn't worry about the concert yet. If you don't hurry, you'll be late for breakfast, and then you'll have an awful rush to get through before your dancing classes."

Gemma looked at the clock. "Dancing class! My goodness, I'd forgotten in some ways it's an ordinary Saturday, so I've got Ted after dancing, but I'm missing tap this afternoon because Aunt Alice said we were all to rest."

Lydia got off the bed. "Pity it's tap you've got to miss. I think our dance is better than it was at that first concert, but boy, it still needs a lot of work."

Of course, the morning did pass as mornings do on even the most important occasion, and then it was lunchtime. Alice knew the children would be too excited to eat much just before the concert so she gave them lunch food they were sure to enjoy: roast chicken with everything that goes with it, followed by ice cream. After lunch she said: "Gran is going to help me wash up, for I want you all to lie down for a bit."

Robin was disgusted. "Not me, Mom. I don't need to lie down to get ready to play two tunes which I've swirled myself."

"You, too," said Philip. "You may be playing only two tunes, but we'll be lucky if we're home by ten o'clock, and tomorrow is Sunday. Imagine what we shall feel like if we hear you were caught sleeping in your choir stall tomorrow."

Although they all said they wouldn't sleep a wink, surprisingly they all did, and the next thing they knew it was teatime. The wait after tea was awful. The clock seemed to stand still. It felt as if

Philip would never get out the car, but at last it was time to go.

"Come on, Alice, I'm taking you and Gemma and Sisters first." He turned to Gran. "I'll be back soon for you and Robin."

Alice, managing to look much calmer than she felt, helped the three girls to dress. Then Gemma put a little rouge on all their cheeks, some powder on their noses, and they all used a pale lipstick.

Then Alice went around with a brush and comb. They had washed their hair for the occasion, and she thought proudly how nice they looked. Gemma's long fair hair always did look lovely, and so as a rule did Lydia's curls, but that evening she was particularly proud of Ann, for to make a slight difference, her hair was done up on the top of her head, kept in place with a black bow.

Alice gave her a kiss. "You do look nice, darling,"

"Absolutely smashing," said Lydia. "Honestly, Ann, almost I wouldn't know you were you."

"You ought to wear it like that always," Gemma suggested.

Ann was appalled. "Goodness, no! It takes ages." But privately she was pleased with her new hairstyle. *I look*, she thought, *almost as pretty as the others*.

The family came on about halfway through the program. In plenty of time Philip shepherded Nigs and his drums to the right entrance and saw Lydia put her shoes, apron, and scarf on a table.

"Good luck, all," he said cheerfully. "They sound like a good audience. This should be fun."

And it was fun. There was a round of applause as the girls ran on. Luckily Philip was in time to stop Robin from playing the opening music until it died down. Then, Gemma on one side of Ann and Lydia on the other, they sang about the old woman whose skirts were cut up to her knee, with magnificent drum support from Nigs on the Fol, lol, did-dle, did-dle dols.

The audience was enchanted, but before anyone could start to clap, Philip was on the piano stool and Gemma and Lydia were doing their tap dance. This took them both offstage at the end so

36

that Lydia could change for her jig. Gemma ran behind the stage to help her and to collect her collar to put on the piano for her to change back into after her dance.

All this time Ann was singing quite beautifully "Bless This House." Gemma thought, It's almost as if the audience were letting Ann's singing soak into them like rain.

The applause after Ann's song burst like a storm, but Philip would not allow it to go on too long before he played a chord to start Lydia's jig. Gemma, who was also back onstage, leaned against the piano.

How well she dances, she thought. *Oh, dear, I wish I'd finished singing about that horrible lady and her swine. I'm a letdown after the others, I can't help being.*

But Gemma was not a letdown. She was different. She clearly had not the talent of the other two, but she knew how to hold an audience, and there was her wistful quality, which even when she sang a little nursery rhyme brought a lump into a lot of throats.

Then Ann and Lydia slipped forward, and Ann led them in "Oh, Dear, What Can the Matter Be?" Then they held hands and bowed all at the same time, as Gemma had taught them, and their part of the concert was over. But not quite, for Nigs, coached by his father, left his drums and came forward and presented each of the girls with a bouquet.

Those bouquets really were cherries on the top of the cake.

"Us being given bouquets!" Lydia gasped. "It's the grandest thing that ever happened."

Then, at home over supper, each item of their program had to be discussed. Gran was like a fat tabby cat who has drunk a bottle full of cream.

"They say listeners never hear any good of themselves, but you should have heard some of the nice things being said around us."

"It's true, darlings, you were a tremendous success," said Alice, "but you must have known that by the applause."

Robin bounced on his seat. "I knew it. Right away from my first song. They liked my swirled music."

"You hurry up eating," said Philip, "or the master won't like your singing in church tomorrow." Then he turned to Gemma. "What you've got to think about, Gemma, is encores."

"They actually called 'encore' after your song, Ann," said Gran.

"I think," Philip said, "they would have encored all three of you, but as Ann didn't sing again, they could see they wouldn't get it."

"Encores!" Gemma's mind was already working. "It would take a bit of planning, but I suppose it could be managed."

"Don't worry tonight, darling," said Alice. "I do want you all to get quickly to sleep, so if you'll hurry up, I'll put your flowers in water."

Lydia looked fondly at her bouquet, "Miss Lydie Robinson is seeing the day when you won't be able to get into her dressing room for all the flowers in it."

They laughed but at the same time wondered if perhaps Lydia's dream might come true.

Gran shook her head at her. "You be careful, Lydie. Don't count your chickens before they are hatched."

Gemma shivered.

"Are you cold, darling?" Alice asked.

Gemma shook her head.

"Just reaction I suppose, but when Mrs. Robinson said that, I felt a goose walk over my grave."

8 ❧ Christmas

THIS TIME there was no need for Gemma to grumble that no one had heard of Gemma and Sisters. The parents of many of the pupils at school and some of the children had been at the concert and had carried home the news of the success of Gemma and Sisters. By Monday the school was buzzing with it, and even a sixth-former, who was head of class 3's house, came to congratulate Ann.

"My mother says you were ever so good. 'Quite professional,' she said. If you could make money for a school charity like our guide dogs for the blind, you might get some house marks."

The school was grouped into houses called after famous authors. The house with the highest number of points won in any year won the House Cup. To Ann house marks mattered terribly, so she flushed with pleasure.

"Oh, thanks awfully. I'll see what I can do."

Gemma was charmed at the family's notoriety, and as always, when her ego was satisfied, she was at her best. Ann, who had noticed this, took advantage of it. On the way home she tackled Gemma about house marks, though knowing Gemma could not care less which house won the cup.

"House Captain spoke to me today." She gave a slight pause, in case Gemma made appropriate sounds of respect and admiration at such an unusual occurrence, but nothing was forthcoming, so she went on. "She had heard about Gemma and Sisters, and she said if we did something for a school charity like the guide dogs, we could earn house marks. I suppose," Ann went on, carried away by the glory of the idea, "dozens of house marks if we earned enough to buy a whole dog."

Gemma was totally unimpressed by house marks but—though she could not see how it could be done—charmed at the idea of a full-length performance.

"It will want a lot of working out, and we couldn't do it until Christmas is over, but then, if we all worked, we might—we really might."

Even Gran was satisfied with the excitement caused by the Winter Garden concert. The Headstone papers really went to town over it, each mentioning that the performers were all, with one exception, from one local family, the Robinsons; the exception was not Gemma but Nigs. Gemma didn't mind. If she was going to appear as an amateur, she wanted to be accepted as Robinson, but she was pleased that as Gemma Robinson her song was noticed, though not raved about like Ann's singing or Lydia's dancing.

Miss Arrowhead had not been present at the concert. She knew if she were in the audience, sharp eyes would spot her, and Rosie Glesse's mom would not be the only one to demand that her child should dance in public if Lydia were allowed to.

"You know, Polly, as we haven't time to rehearse each individually, and I can't have my pupils appearing in public unrehearsed, I think I'll give a public performance in the summer and use them all."

They were eating supper when Miss Arrowhead said this, and Polly was so surprised that she choked and had to be revived by thumps on the back.

"Glory!" she said when she could speak. "I never thought I'd hear you say a thing like that. What sort of public performance? A little ballet or individual turns?"

"A sort of ballet," Miss Arrowhead explained. "That is to say, the whole performance held together by a slight story. Probably a fairy story in a magic wood because then we can use the babies as rabbits and so on."

"With the principal fairy danced by Lydie?"

Miss Arrowhead shook her head. "No. That is the idea behind the enterprise. All the school will take part except Lydie."

"But she's your star pupil."

"Already appearing in public. So, without saying so, I shall let it be understood I prefer my children, if they dance in public, to dance for me. I think the lesson will sink home, and we shall find there will be no more requests for individual performances."

Lydia soon picked up news of Miss Arrowhead's public performance. Hints were dropped to each parent who had either seen Lydia dance at the Winter Garden or read her notices in the papers and asked if in future they could accept invitations for her child. To each Miss Arrowhead said: "It's a secret at the moment, but in the summer I am giving a public show, and I would like"—Shirley, Rosie, Hayley, or Mary, according to which proud mom she was speaking—"to be fresh for that."

Lydia tried to worm news out of Miss Arrowhead, but of course, she got none. She just looked at Lydia down her long, sharp nose and said: "You've got enough on your plate for the moment. Let's get the Serbian dance right before we start thinking about next year."

Lydia didn't care, for she knew the answer. She was the star pupil, so of course, she would have a star part. She wouldn't be allowed to dance on her pointes like the big girls, for she had only just been elevated to blocked shoes, but it was sure to be a glorious part; she might even wear a proper ballet dress.

In the meantime, Lydia was too busy to worry. Requests for Gemma and Sisters had rolled in and not only from Headstone but from places outside the town: Christmas parties for old people; a party in the Town Hall the mayor was giving for cripples. There was no end to it.

"Each of you must have an encore for these types of concerts," Philip said. "The old people particularly are sure to expect each of you to perform twice. It will be their Christmas outing, and they'll like a long entertainment."

"Then I better swirl some more songs," said Robin, "so if the girls get extra claps at the end after their bows, they can sing an extra song. I'll choose one so Nigs can use his drums."

Soon the house was ringing with Robin's latest effort: "Aiken Drum."

> There was a man lived in the moon,
> lived in the moon, lived in the moon,
> There was a man lived in the moon,
> And his name was Ai-ken Drum.

"And this one," Robin stated, "needs Nigs's drums all the way through."

"You can all learn all the encores you like," said Alice, "and you can swirl as many songs as you like, Robin, but I insist on one thing; Christmas Day is to be just Christmas Day—no rehearsals, no anything, just blessed Christmas."

Outwardly that was just what Christmas Day was, though nobody could stop what was thought. Gemma was particularly bursting with thoughts, not only about Gemma and Sisters but about something Miss Jenkins had said to her on the last day of the term. Miss Jenkins, though she taught English, specialized in drama, so coached the drama group. "I am hoping to have some exciting news for you next term, Gemma. It's time we worked on a new play."

Exciting news! What play? A proper play in the school hall? The drama group produced a play now and again. This time, if it was exciting news, it must be a leading part for her. Gemma hugged herself. She'd show the school what she could do. Not just the child in a pageant but real acting.

Gemma had learned when she came to live with the cousins that Christmas in Trelawny Drive was something she knew nothing about. It started early when they designed and made their own Christmas cards. Then came present buying, no casual going to a big store and choosing a lot of things, such as she and her mother had done, but careful listening and watching to find out what everybody really needed.

Then there were decorations: some made at home and some bought but all put up by the whole family.

Then the tree arrived. It stood in the hall and was decorated on Christmas Eve by Philip and Alice when the children were in bed, so none of them saw it in its shimmering glory until Christmas Day.

For Gemma Christmas began when a stupendous box arrived from her mother full of presents all beautifully gift-wrapped by the shops. It could not be said that the contents of the parcels were always just what everybody wanted, for it is difficult to choose presents when you live far away. But opening her mother's box and laying out the parcels had become part of Christmas. This year the presents had been bought early, for Gemma's mother was on location in a desert. "So I shall not," she had written, "get my Christmas letters and parcels until the first week in the New Year."

Christmas Day was just as Alice wanted it to be. Lydia, Gemma, and Philip walked to church together calling out "Merry Christmas" to all the passersby. Ann, when she marched in with the choir, looked lovely in her blue cassock and three-cornered blue velvet hat, and she sang the solo "Sweet Was the Song the Virgin Sang" most beautifully.

When they got home, Alice had the Christmas table laid and the turkey ready to serve.

"And though I say it as shouldn't, the plum pudding looks perfect," she said.

Washing up done, they gathered around the tree to undo the presents: a spellbinding time which carried them on until tea. Then there was carol singing around the fire and supper for those who had room for it.

"But," said Lydia as she went up to bed, "although this has been an absolutely perfect day, nobody can say nothing nice will ever happen again, so much is happening and all of it glorious."

Gemma again felt as if cold feet were walking down her back. It was true everything looked perfect, but she did wish Lydia wouldn't sort of brag about it.

9 ❧ Long Distance

AFTER SO MUCH excitement in the Christmas holidays it seemed dull to be getting back into uniform for the start of the new term. Still, for each of the girls there were compensations, and even Robin admitted he would be glad of more spare time. "With all the concerts we've been giving I haven't had proper time to swirl anything new; now I can really get down to it."

"But not at the expense of your schoolwork, I hope," said Philip. "Don't forget St. Giles expects a high standard of work as well as of singing from its scholars."

"Don't flap," Robin retorted. "I can work and swirl. I always have."

Philip's eye twinkled. "Well, watch it. In your last term's report there were two 'could do betters.'"

"Don't fuss about that," said Robin. "Masters just write that when they can't think of anything else to say."

Ann, though she had secretly found the concerts more fun than singing alone, was glad they were over for the time being. There was a new good singing teacher at Headstone School of Music, and Philip had decided Ann should have lessons. This, though it would be hard to fit in with her school and choirwork, made the term look exciting.

"I think you may have to give up your school choir," Philip had suggested.

Ann had been shocked at the suggestion. "I couldn't. I get house marks every term for singing in it."

Philip laughed. "I am sorry about the house marks, but whether you do or do not sing in choirs will be up to your teacher to decide."

Ann nodded, but privately she was certain she could talk the singing teacher around.

For once Gemma went cheerfully back to school. She was longing to hear what plans Miss Jenkins had for her.

Lydia was not keen to go back to school, and she was sorry the concerts were over, but there was Miss Arrowhead's public performance to look forward to.

I'm sure to have the best part, she thought happily, *and rehearsals will be fun. Oh, I do hope I wear a ballet dress.*

The first to hear news was Gemma. Miss Jenkins sent for her after school. She was waiting in a little office the staff used when they wanted to talk privately with anyone.

Miss Jenkins was a small, willowy woman with fair hair worn drooping over her cheeks and fastened in a bun in the nape of her neck. She was rather intense but had a real love for the theater and was becoming quite a good producer. She gave Gemma a welcoming smile. "Sit down, dear. What do you know about Lady Jane Grey, Gemma?"

Gemma, being fond of history, knew a little, but she had to think hard to dig it out of her memory.

"She was the great-granddaughter of Henry the Seventh, and, because of that, when Henry the Eighth's son Edward the Sixth died, her father, who was a lord—I forget which—had her proclaimed queen. She was called queen for only nine days and then she was put in the Tower, and there Queen Mary had her beheaded, which I have always thought pretty mean, for it wasn't her fault she was called queen; it was her father's."

"Very good," said Miss Jenkins. "Her father was the marquess of Dorset, afterward the duke of Suffolk. He arranged a marriage for Jane when she was only sixteen to the duke of Northumberland's son, Lord Guilford Dudley."

45

"Oh, I knew that, but I'd forgotten him," Gemma said. "And he was beheaded too. I think Jane saw him beheaded from her window in the Tower because he was done first."

"Do you know any more about her? About her education?"

Gemma searched her memory. "I'm afraid not."

On the table in front of Miss Jenkins a manuscript was lying. Miss Jenkins picked it up.

"I have always been fond of Lady Jane Grey. So last year I attempted to write a play about her. I really only did it for fun and because of my interest in her. I never dreamed my play would be produced. Then last term I showed it to Mr. Weldon, and he worked with me on it. Then he read it to those who run the drama group, and as a result, it is to be produced for three performances in May."

Mr. Weldon was the English teacher who had written the pageant, so Gemma knew what it must have meant to have his approval.

"My goodness!" said Gemma. "It's smashing for you."

Miss Jenkins looked for a moment not much older than Jane. "Isn't it! I'm thrilled. But it has presented casting difficulties—very great casting difficulties. You see, when we first see Jane, she is only ten—that is where she hears of the death of Henry the Eighth—and when we last see her, she is sixteen. So no one actress could be right for the whole part, but we have decided that with the help of the costumes we can probably get over the age difficulty, and most of the play Lady Jane is in her early teens."

Gemma's mind whirled. Early teens! Just like her! What a part! Was Miss Jenkins going to say she had been chosen to play it?

"When you say she is sixteen, is that when her head is cut off?"

"That's right. She puts her head on the block and the ax is raised just as the curtain falls."

"Goodness!" Gemma whispered. "What a part! What a stupendous part!"

"It is," Miss Jenkins said. "And we all are agreed you should play it, but there are great difficulties. Lady Jane was a startlingly well-educated girl; she was considered a marvel even in an age

46

when aristocratic girls were well educated. She spoke and wrote Greek and Latin, and she does in the play, and she had a smattering of some Oriental languages as well. That has been our casting difficulty; nobody I think could say you were a marvel from an educational point of view. You have learned neither Greek nor Latin, have you?"

Gemma clasped her hands.

"No, I haven't, but I must act her; it sounds like a glorious part. I'm not a bit worried about speaking Greek and Latin, I'll slave and slave until I get it right. Honestly you can't think how I'll work so as not to let you down."

Miss Jenkins handed Gemma the manuscript. To her, parting with a copy of her play was obviously like parting with a baby.

"Take it home, and read it. But be honest with yourself; be absolutely sure you can manage it before you decide. It is not easy to speak Latin or Greek when you have studied neither, though you will, of course, be coached. By the way, for the time being you are not to mention this play to anybody."

Gemma walked home in a daze. Lady Jane Grey! How simply glorious! She saw herself blindfolded, laying her head on the block while the whole school sobbed. Then suddenly she was conscious Ann was talking. "I said I'd see what I could do, but it won't be easy now I'm having singing lessons. Still, we'd get a lot of house marks if we did it."

It was no use pretending.

"Did what?" Gemma asked.

Ann looked at her with disgust. "Haven't you listened to a word? House Captain came to me. Imagine! She asked point-blank if Gemma and Sisters would do a whole show to buy a dog for the blind. But Dad thinks I may be stopped singing solos now I'm learning properly."

Gemma had to push Lady Jane Grey to the back of her mind. "If you can't sing, we can't do another Gemma and Sisters at all."

"We could learn some songs we could sing together. I'd be allowed to do that, I should think."

47

Gemma was firm. "If you can't sing, the show is off until you can."

Ann looked at her curiously. "You don't sound as though you care. I thought you'd be in a state about it."

Gemma thought of the manuscript of the play in her schoolbag, which was hanging on her shoulder.

"I heard Uncle Philip talking to Aunt Alice about it. He only said you might not be allowed to use your voice at first, but he didn't think it would be long because, as far as he could see, you had no bad habits."

"Oh, good! Well, if I can sing, will you think about the dog for the blind concert?"

Gemma wanted nothing except to get home and read the play. "All right," she said. "That'll be okay."

There was never much homework on the first day of the term, so Gemma, curled up on her bed, was able to bury herself in the play. Dimly she heard Aunt Alice come home. Subconsciously she registered Uncle Philip was home. Miles away the telephone rang. Uncle Philip seemed to be shouting into it. Then her name was called.

"Gemma! Gemma! Come down, it's your mother talking from California. It's an awful line, but I gather she thinks you are unhappy at Headstone Consolidated. We are to find you a new school tomorrow; she doesn't mind what it costs."

10 ౿ Mr. Stevens

GEMMA HAD, when she had been called to the telephone, been Lady Jane Grey. She was feeling like her, almost thinking like her except that Lady Jane, as Miss Jenkins had said, was so much more clever than she was. Although she had to skip the dialogue where she was studying Latin or Greek with her tutor, she saw no difficulties ahead. Of course, she would act the part; it was as certain as that the sun would rise in the morning.

It was not a bit like taking to her mother yelling across the Atlantic, for though she could hear what her mother said, her mother did not seem able to hear her or, if she did, to take in what she was saying. It was all such nonsense.

"That sounds like a ghastly school. Only just got your letter or I would have done something before. How dare they put you in the bottom stream? Miss Court said you were brilliant. You are to leave right away and must have a governess until a suitable school that can appreciate you is found."

Gemma tried to make her mother understand. "I didn't mean I hated the school. Actually I love it. I didn't mean what I said; it was just a mood," and finally: "I won't leave, Mommy. I tell you I won't."

At the end of the conversation Gemma crossly slammed down the telephone. Since she had lived in Headstone, there had been other transatlantic telephone calls for birthdays and at Christmas, but they had all been "Lovely to hear your voice"; "How are you, darling?" sort of talk, never an argument or orders from her mother. The telephone was in the hall. She came into the living room scowling.

"I don't know what's bitten Mommy, going off the handle like that. But I tell you one thing, I'm not leaving Headstone Consolidated whatever she says."

The family was surprised, for they had never thought Gemma liked the school particularly. Philip said: "I'm afraid it is not for you to decide. If your mother wants to send you to a different type of school, then we must find one, and temporarily we must find you a governess."

Gemma was horrified. She could almost see Lady Jane floating out of the window. She turned to Alice. "Aunt Alice, you know Mommy. She gets in a state about things in a second; by the next day she doesn't remember anything about it."

Alice turned to Philip. "It's quite true, and anyway, it's nonsense talking about getting a governess tomorrow; of course, we couldn't. I doubt if there is a private governess in the whole of Headstone."

"So I must go on at Headstone Consolidated for a bit, anyway," Gemma pointed out. "I'll write Mommy a long letter tomorrow explaining. Honestly, Uncle Philip, it's all a flap about nothing. I promise you it is."

But Philip was not sure. "Your mother is quite right about one thing; you have been bogged down too long in that bottom stream. I daresay you would be better in a small private school, and if she doesn't mind paying—"

Alice saw difficulties. "But no private school is going to take Gemma without notice."

"I don't know so much," said Philip. "I don't believe that school up by the park has begun a new term yet. You could see the headmistress tomorrow."

"Gosh!" gasped Lydia. "That is the poshest school in the town. Imagine you going there, Gemma!"

Gemma saw she had to fight. "I won't go anywhere except to the

50

Consolidated. Please do wait until I have an answer to my letter to Mommy."

Alice was entirely on Gemma's side. She had no wish to start shopping for a different uniform and all the other things a new and rather grand school would demand. She saw other troubles ahead as well. The school by the park, if it took Gemma, was a long way off; how was the child to get to and fro? There was no direct bus service. It would be all right for Ann to go across Headstone alone because she was her own child, but Gemma was in her charge and, incidentally, nothing like as sensible as Ann.

"I think Gemma's talking sense, Philip," she said. "Let her write to her mother—and airmail the letter, Gemma. If in answer she still insists on a new school, we must see who will take her at half term. But it's ridiculous rushing around now when Rowena may have changed her mind in a couple of days."

Unwillingly Philip agreed. "Very well. But I shall start tomorrow inquiring about schools. It will do no harm to find out what there are."

Upset by the telephone conversation, though Gemma read the rest of the play before she went to bed, she never again got quite so lost in it. All the same she had tears in her eyes when she read the last page. The stage directions said: "She kneels with her arms outstretched. Her head is on the block. Lady Jane: 'Lord, into Thy hands I commend my spirit.' "

CURTAIN

Only sixteen and a half, thought Gemma, and she felt humble. *If I get a chance to act her, how I hope I make people care what happened to her.*

The next day Gemma saw Miss Jenkins.

"I think it's wonderful," Gemma said. "I know it will be difficult because of the Latin and the Greek, but more than anything in the world I want to act her."

Miss Jenkins told her to keep her copy of the play. "If you can master the Latin and Greek scenes, you shall. You might start learning the first scene right away."

In the lunch break Gemma wrote to her mother. She implored her not to fuss. She told her about Lady Jane.

"But if you are writing to Aunt Alice, don't mention the play because it's a secret. So you see, even if you want me to go to another school, I couldn't until after the play, and honestly, honestly I don't want to move. I like it at Headstone Consolidated."

That ought to calm things down, she thought as she licked up the edges of the airmail letter.

That afternoon a girl from another class brought Gemma a message that she was to see Mr. Stevens after school. Gemma felt physically sick. The headmaster seldom saw his pupils and certainly nothing so low in school life as a girl in 3G. If he was seeing her, it must be because there had been another message from her mother, and she really was being sent to a different school. But she would not move. She knew her letter would change her mother's mind, and so she would tell Mr. Stevens.

All through afternoon lessons she turned over at the back of her head what she would say to Mr. Stevens. She had to keep her thoughts to the back because she did not want any more trouble about inattention.

As soon as school was over, she shoved her schoolbooks and the precious copy of the play into her bag, asked one of the class to tell Ann not to wait for her, then set off with her head high but very tremulous inside for Mr. Stevens's office.

Mr. Stevens was young for a headmaster. He had a good classical degree and loved teaching. Though he was glad to have been chosen for his position, he wished his duties did not give him as much time as he would like to teach. He was a good-looking man with dark hair and deep-set gray eyes.

Mr. Stevens, in spite of Gemma's lowly position in the school, had met her before. He had never forgotten the meeting because of the way Gemma had engineered it. Outside his door was a large black chair known as the punishment chair. A boy or girl had to behave extraordinarily badly to be sent to sit in the chair, and even big boys quailed at the thought. Mostly it was because of the humiliation. Whoever sat in the chair could be seen by the whole school, and when Mr. Stevens came out of his office, the telling-off for whatever sin had been committed was heard by all who were passing by. But Gemma, who had decided the only way to get into the drama group was through her headmaster, had calmly walked up to the punishment chair and sat in it, knowing he must speak to her there. In any event, as Mr. Stevens admitted to his staff, Gemma had done quite right to fight to get into the drama group, as the pageant had proved. Now, as she came in, he smiled at her. "Sit down, Gemma."

But Gemma was too fussed to sit. "You mustn't pay any attention to what my mother wants. When she's read my letter, she'll see about Lady Jane Grey and—"

Mr. Stevens held up his hand. "Sit down. I've no idea what you are talking about except about Lady Jane."

"Oh!" Gemma sat, feeling rather like a balloon out of which all the air is escaping. "I'm sorry. You see, I thought if you were seeing somebody as low as me, it must be because of a message from my mother—perhaps even a cable because she's in America."

Mr. Stevens leaned on his desk. "Now calm down. What I wanted to see you about is this play. A very fine effort on Miss Jenkins's part, and I agree with the drama group that you are the best choice to act the part. But there is the Latin and Greek problem, and there perhaps I can help. There is one scene, as you know, where Jane speaks Latin and another where she speaks Greek. The question is, could you, if I coached you, master these scenes? Both languages must be spoken correctly and fluently."

Gemma was quite sure of herself. "That'll be all right. In a"—she was going to say "film," but she broke off in time— "play—you remember I told you I'd acted a lot—well, in one I had to speak Chinese, which is awfully hard, but they got a Chinese to teach me, and I learned all right."

"Did you indeed! Well, we must see if I am as efficient as the Chinese coach. Miss Jenkins will arrange for you to come to me when I can spare you half an hour."

The interview was evidently over. Gemma got up. "Thanks awfully. I'll love learning with you."

Mr. Stevens stared at the door. Ever since he had first met Gemma, her voice had haunted him, for he was sure he had heard it in some other connection. Now he was amused by her manner, the way she had said, "I'll love learning with you."

It is almost, he thought, *as if she expected me to be gratified that she is pleased. What an extraordinary child!*

11 ❦ Trouble for Lydia

GEMMA WAS NOT the only one to write to Rowena. Alice also wrote. Hers was a sensible sister-to-sister letter. She reminded Rowena that girls of thirteen were apt to get in a state about nothing at all—didn't we all? she said, and added:

> You lived in a permanent state at that age. I don't for one second believe Gemma is unhappy at school. I would know if she was. She is not the academic type, nor ever will be, but neither were you. We do want her to work a little harder so she gets into the middle stream; this would be the right place for her; she's working below her capacity where she is. Her stumbling block is math, but so was yours. If you remember, you were still adding on your fingers when you left school, and it wouldn't surprise me if you were still at it. I do wish you could hear Gemma singing to her accompaniment on her banjo. She looks exquisite, and there is a quality about her which brings a lump into my throat every time I hear her.

The result of the two letters was that Rowena first cabled and then wrote to say that for the time being Gemma might stay where she was. "Later on," she said, "I have plans for her."

55

Later on was one of those elastic terms like *sometime* or *someday*; it meant nothing, so nobody worried about it.

"Thank goodness," Alice said to Philip, "now we can settle down to a peaceful term."

Alice spoke without any idea of what Lydia was going to hear that afternoon.

It was one of the days when Lydia had her private lesson with Miss Arrowhead after school. She went to the changing room to put on her tunic and shoes and the regulation band around her hair. In the changing room she found Rosie Glesse dressing to go home.

"Hello!" said Lydia. "I didn't know you had a lesson today."

"I don't ordinarily," Rosie explained, "but my mom is paying for me to have some extra classes with Polly. Well, I asked her if I could really—you see, Mom thinks I'll be marvelous in Miss Arrowhead's show, but I'm scared to death to dance a solo."

Lydia was not upset by this news; she supposed she would hear after her lesson what role she was to dance.

"What sort of dance is it?"

"Well, it's in the magic wood; I'm a foxglove. There are several flowers, and we all have different dances."

Lydia sat on the floor to tie the ribbons on her shoes. "I wouldn't fuss. You won't be alone on the stage, will you?"

"Goodness, no. That would scare me so I should think I'd fall flat on my face. No, it's Mom. She truly thinks I'm going to be much better than anyone else."

Lydia privately marveled at Rosie's being given a solo to dance, for she didn't think her much of a dancer. But she liked Rosie, so she tried to cheer her up. "It'll be all right, you'll see, and I bet you have a gorgeous dress."

Rosie nodded. "That's the best part of it. It's a green tutu, and I have a foxglove flower on my head."

"A green tutu! Aren't you lucky! I'd love to wear one of those."

"I expect you will," said Rosie. "What are you dancing? Is it the spirit of the wood? When Miss Arrowhead told us about the ballet, we all guessed you would be the spirit."

Lydia got up and straightened her tunic. "I'm going to my lesson now. I shall hear then. Wish me luck that I wear a tutu."

Miss Arrowhead never allowed talking before classes. She smiled at Lydia. "Good afternoon, dear. Go to the barre."

Lydia was far too absorbed in what she was doing to let her mind wander during classes, but the moment Miss Arrowhead said, "That will be all for today, Lydie," she made her curtsy and then danced eagerly across the studio to where Miss Arrowhead was standing.

"Rosie Glesse was telling me about being a foxglove in your show and how she's going to wear a tutu."

Miss Arrowhead nodded. "I'm trying to see that those rather expensive dresses are worn by those whose parents can easily afford to buy them."

With a sigh Lydia said good-bye to a tutu. Obviously she wouldn't rank as somebody whose parents were rich. Then she cheered up. It was the dancing that mattered, not really what you wore.

"What am I going to be?"

Miss Arrowhead spoke very gently. "You aren't going to be in my show, Lydie. You are already dancing in Gemma and Sisters, and the preparations for your solos for that take quite enough time from your studies as it is. I couldn't allow you to take on anything more."

Lydia could not believe what Miss Arrowhead was saying. Slowly her face turned crimson.

"Have a public performance without me! You couldn't, you simply couldn't. All the girls say I'm the best dancer."

"You are my best pupil from the point of view of promise; you have in fact more promise than any child I have so far taught. If my hopes for you come true, there is nowhere you could not go. But a successful future comes from steady hard work, not from dancing in special matinees."

To her annoyance Lydia found herself crying. "It's mean. You're punishing me because I danced that first time in Gemma and Sisters without telling you."

57

"No, Lydie, this is not a punishment. It's in a way a compliment. I think too much of your talent to waste it."

"No one is going to believe that." Lydia sobbed. "They're all expecting me to dance the wood spirit. Rosie told me so."

"Don't cry, dear," said Miss Arrowhead. "You can tell the girls what I've said. In fact, if I get an opportunity, I shall tell them myself. Now run along, I have a group coming to rehearse."

Lydia went to the changing room, which was mercifully empty. She pulled off her tunic and shoes and dragged on her outdoor clothes, all the time muttering under her breath, "It's mean. It's mean. I don't care what she says, it's a punishment. I know it's a punishment."

Ann had just started the children's tea when Lydia stormed in. Ann saw her tearstained face and half got out of her chair. "What's up?"

With more tears streaming down her face Lydia poured out her sad story, finishing with "And Rosie Glesse, who dances as if she were made of wood, is wearing a green tutu with a foxglove on her head."

"What a shame!" Ann said kindly. "But I do see what Miss Arrowhead means: Your lessons are more important than learning dances for a matinee."

Lydia sat down. "You can say what you like, but I'm not going to give in. I'll show Miss Arrowhead what happens when she's mean to me."

"How?" asked Robin, who was always interested in rebellion.

"I'm not sure yet," said Lydia, "but because of my dancing, I've always taken care not to do things that use wrong muscles. Well, now I'll do all the wrong things. And every morning I do twelve grands pliés before breakfast; well, I won't do them anymore."

Ann felt sure Lydia was just letting off steam, so she spoke gently. "Have a talk to Dad when he gets home. He'll make you see you mustn't do anything to hurt your dancing; you know really you wouldn't."

"All the same it is bad luck," said Gemma. "I know just how she feels."

But Lydia did not want sympathy. "I shan't talk to Dad or anyone. I'll show Miss Arrowhead she can't treat me like that, and you'll see in the end I'll win."

12 ❧ A Bicycle

IT WAS unfortunate from Lydia's point of view that Hugo Forrest, Ann's singing teacher at the School of Music, put his foot down about solos. He said: "It will be for only a short time, but I want us to work together on exercises for the next couple of months. You have not hurt your voice singing at concerts, for your father is quite right when he says you have no harmful faults, but until the end of the year solo singing is out."

Ann did not care; she looked forward to her lessons and to understanding how she should produce her voice. "But it's bad luck on Lydie," she told her father. "I mean, if we had some Gemma and Sisters concerts lined up for now, she wouldn't be so mad at missing Miss Arrowhead's public performances next year. Still, it isn't long to wait until January, and we'll be doing a lot of concerts then."

It was no longer a secret that Miss Jenkins's play was being produced in May and that Gemma—if she could manage the Latin and Greek—was to play Lady Jane. The drama group had been told, and casting of the other parts was going on, so of course, the news was common school gossip.

"It makes it extra hard for Lydie," said Philip, "that Gemma, who in the ordinary way would be working in every way she knew to rehearse for next year's concerts for Gemma and Sisters, is so wrapped up in Lady Jane she can think of nothing else."

Ann nodded. "No wonder she had a fit when Aunt Rowena wanted her to change schools."

It was a black period for Lydia. She felt more miserable each time she went to the studio. There always seemed to be somebody being coached, and wherever she looked there were designs for dresses lying about with snippets of materials pinned to them. Worse still, even though she missed her daily pliés and tried her hardest to do things that pulled her muscles the wrong way, there was no noticeable change in her dancing. At least, if there was, Miss Arrowhead didn't say anything about it.

Then one day in bed Lydia had a new idea. She thought it would be fun to do, and it just might make Miss Arrowhead see she could be just as tough as she was. At each dancing class she would stop being herself and instead give a really good imitation of Miss Arrowhead's worst dancers. *I'll do all of them*, she decided, *especially Rosie Glesse.*

It did not take Miss Arrowhead one lesson to spot what Lydia was up to. Secretly, though she was annoyed, she was also amused. But she kept a straight face, said nothing, and waited for Lydia to find out for herself that she was wasting her time. She was being a tiresome child, but patience would win.

Patience did not win, and when a second week passed and not once did the real Lydia show through her impersonations, Miss Arrowhead had to think again.

"That bad little Lydie is getting me down," she told Polly. "Imitating inferior dancers is not doing her work any good, especially when she imitates the all too many who stick out their posteriors in every exercise."

Polly laughed. "I bet she's funny."

"Very"—Miss Arrowhead agreed—"but I feel like Queen Victoria—'We are not amused.' I'm afraid I'm going to let Lydia win."

"You can't," Polly protested. "She'll think she can get away with anything."

Miss Arrowhead sighed. "The truth is she can if only she will work. Anyway, what I have in mind is just as much for my sake as for hers. You know how our horrid little ballet fizzles out badly at

61

the end. Well, I was thinking, for the curtain, we could fix the lights so that we get the effect of night falling on the wood."

"Pretty music," said Polly, "and all the rabbits, flowers, fairies, et cetera, falling asleep. The moms will adore it. But where does Lydie come in?"

"I thought she could be a fairy of sorts—it will be she who puts them all to sleep. It's a good idea to startle the audience by keeping my best dancer to the end."

"When are you going to tell Lydie?"

"Not yet, and anyway, I'm not promising her the part. She's going to get a good telling off first with a threat of no more private lessons, and then I'll hint that if she works, there may be a part for her."

"Very clever," said Polly, "but make the ticking off tough; young Lydie gets away with too much."

Lydia, having no idea what Miss Arrowhead was planning, was getting desperate. For once she was not getting her own way. Of course, Miss Arrowhead must see she wasn't working properly, and she would know why, but she wasn't giving in. Lydia poured out her troubles to Robin. He was not her first choice of confidant; she would have much preferred Gemma, but Gemma was no use to anyone now because every spare minute she was learning Lady Jane.

Robin was more sympathetic than Lydia had expected. The reason was both he and Nigs were feeling badly done by because, owing to Ann, there were no concerts until January for Gemma and Sisters.

"I do know how you feel, because me and Nigs are awfully browned off with no new songs to swirl and for him to play the drums. I know Dad says there are lots in January, but that's ages away. When I swirl something, I like it to be rehearsed now."

"Then imagine me," said Lydia. "No Gemma and Sisters and no rehearsals for the public performance. It isn't fair. Everybody else is dancing. Imagine leaving me out!"

"Won't she come around?" Robin suggested. "I mean, whatever the solo boys did, I don't think our teacher would stop them from singing. Well, it wouldn't be sense, would it? After all, he wants the best music he can get, and I should think your old Arrowhead wants the best dancing."

"I'm trying to wear her down so she'll change her mind," Lydia explained. "But I've had no luck so far. I wish I knew what was the very, very worst thing I could do to my muscles. She minds about them."

Robin had an idea. "A boy at school fell downstairs and hurt his back. When it was better, the doctor said he was to swim every day, that was for his muscles."

"I swim with the school already, and anyway, it's good for a dancer. No, it's something much more ferocious I need, like riding a horse."

Robin thought that a splendid idea. "Where will you get a horse?"

"I can't. I only meant that was the sort of exercise I was looking for."

"How about a bike?" Robin suggested. "Ann hardly ever uses hers now. She doesn't ride to school like she used to before Gemma came, and Dad often drives her to her singing things."

A bicycle! Lydia thought about that, and the more she thought, the more she approved of the idea. All that pedaling ought to make the wrong muscles bulge. She could ride Ann's bicycle after a fashion, though she was not supposed to borrow it without permission, and then she might ride it only in Trelawny Drive; she was never allowed on the main roads. Still, she got home from school long before Ann. She could easily bicycle around and around the drive every afternoon.

She smiled at Robin. "Thank you, my boy. Sometimes you have very good ideas."

To Gemma at that time very little was getting through to her from the outside world. She had always been like that over a new part, and Mommy had said with a proud smile that it was the right way for an artist to feel. Miss Court had never been cross when she dreamed about the part during lessons. "Don't worry, dear, we must make allowances for great talent, mustn't we?" But Philip, studying his niece, was not so approving. One evening he caught her alone; he was looking for Alice. "Where's your aunt? She's very late, isn't she?"

Gemma pulled herself away from Lady Jane.

"I was wondering where she was."

Philip lit his pipe. "I'm delighted about Lady Jane, of course, but I do hope it's not distracting your mind from your schoolwork. That telephone call from your mother has brought your position in the school to my mind. I want you to get into the second stream by next autumn; otherwise, I shall advise your mother to move you."

"Move me! But I thought you knew I don't want to move."

"Unless there are signs that your work is improving, you must be moved."

Gemma was horrified. Just after the success she was hoping to have as Lady Jane, to be pushed into a new school where nobody knew she could act would be intolerable.

"I will work harder, truly I will, but don't make me leave Headstone Consolidated. I could give things up to make time for more homework. I was thinking while I'm working at the play, I'll give up my banjo lessons with Ted, and I might give up dancing too. I shan't need it in the play."

They were in the sitting room. Philip sat in an armchair and patted the arm. "Come and sit here." Gemma sat. "In January Ann will be allowed to sing solos again, so I am promising Gemma and Sisters for several concerts. Many of them are for the same people we performed for last year, so you'll need both your banjo and your dancing, for we must give them new material."

"New material!" Gemma gasped. "Oh, no! Actually I was wondering if somehow I could get out of Gemma and Sisters just till the play is over."

"You know you couldn't. You are its mainspring. It's your know-how that makes it the well-produced little show it is."

"But I want to work at Lady Jane."

"And let down a lot of people, including the old, to whom we gave pleasure last year. Wouldn't that be very selfish?"

Gemma's training as a small child had given her no background

64

for a situation like this. Always, when she was working, there had been nothing for herself or anybody else to consider except her and her part in the film. Although she had to behave well, it had been the same at the studio; she was considered in every way. It was, she knew, for the good of the picture that the actors were kept happy and contented; still, it built up a feeling that always the artist must come first. Now here was Uncle Philip saying she had to think of others—to tear herself away from Lady Jane to prepare a new series of Gemma and Sisters. She looked at her uncle, all that was puzzling her showing on her face.

"If you say so, I suppose I'll have to work at Gemma and Sisters, but can't you see that with a part like Lady Jane I feel I ought to work only at her?"

Philip patted her hand. "I know just how you feel, but a break will do you no harm. Believe me, Gemma, when you are grown-up and are working again in the theater, as I'm sure you will, you will find that being part of a team has made you not only a much nicer person but perhaps a better artist."

Philip was going to say more, but at that moment Alice, her face white and green in patches, flung open the door.

"Oh, Philip! It's Lydie. They brought her into the hospital. The policeman said she was on a bicycle—Ann's, I suppose. She rode out of Trelawny Drive without looking, and a car hit her."

Philip's voice was little more than a whisper. "Was she killed?"

Alice came to him. "No, darling. They don't know yet what the damage is. They have a lot of X rays to take, but one thing is certain: She is concussed, and one leg is injured; it's her hip, I think."

One leg injured! Lydia the dancer! Gemma found tears were pouring down her cheeks. She flung her arms around Alice.

"Oh, darling Aunt Alice, I'm so sorry, so terribly sorry."

13 ❧ Move Your Toes

LYDIA WAS very ill for some days, for though the car had hit the bicycle a glancing blow, in falling she had injured her head on the curbstone. Fortunately the car had not been going fast and had swerved to avoid Lydia, but even so, a wheel had hit her.

It was lucky for Alice that she worked in the hospital, for it meant she could have a look at Lydia whenever she wanted to. But for some days there was nothing anyone could do but sit quietly by her bed.

Lydia's accident brought a lot of sympathy. The neighbors, friends, and children from her school were always coming to Trelawny Drive to know how she was and to bring her presents of flowers, fruit, and sweets. The most distressed visitor was Miss Arrowhead. She came around in person to inquire and was greeted by Robin, who was the first home from school. He repeated carefully what they had been told to say. "She is going on all right, but she has to be kept very quiet until her head is better."

"How did the accident happen?" Miss Arrowhead asked.

"Well," said Robin, "it was because of you really—I mean, not letting her dance in your ballet. It was to use the wrong muscles to show you she thought it was mean. She wanted a horse, but as we haven't one, I suggested a bicycle."

Miss Arrowhead was very upset. "Oh, dear! Silly child! I didn't know she had a bicycle."

"She hasn't. It was Ann's she borrowed. Dad says I'm not to bother that I suggested the bicycle because I couldn't know Lydie would ride it in the main road where she's not allowed to go."

"No, it wasn't your fault." Miss Arrowhead agreed. "I suppose if it's anybody's fault, it is mine."

"I wouldn't fuss," said Robin kindly. "Dad says it's nobody's fault but Lydie's."

"I heard she had injured her hip. Is it true?"

"Yes, she's got to stay in bed for six weeks. Her leg is in a pulley thing. Dad says when she comes home, she'll have to use crutches."

"Poor little Lydie! Will you give your mother a message to say how sorry I am and I'll be along to see Lydie as soon as I'm allowed."

In the days immediately after the accident all the family, except Robin, who was remarkably calm, had hard work to get through their ordinary day's work.

"I sang so badly today," Ann told her father, "that I had to tell Mr. Forrest why. He was awfully nice and said he understood, but he told me that if I am good enough to be a professional someday, I shan't be able to let my private life interfere with my singing."

"That's true." Philip agreed. "And quite a help really. Several times these last days I've wished I were back with the orchestra; it's easier to lose yourself in music as a performer than as a teacher."

It was bad luck on Gemma that one of her lessons with Mr. Stevens came on the day after the accident. She was so sure that she would be unable to work well that she told him what had happened.

"And the most awful thing of all is that it is her hip. You see, Lydie is a dancer, a real one; she's going to be good."

Mr. Stevens was kind, but he was not really worried that his time would be wasted. He had from the first lesson he'd given Gemma been amazed at the knowledgeable way in which she worked. He had expected to have to teach her rudiments of Latin and Greek, but he found this was not what she wanted. She asked him to say every word slowly, and she then wrote it down phonetically.

"I'll learn it by heart this way, and then, when I know it perfectly, I'll get you to teach me what it means, so I get the inflections right."

Naturally, as a classical scholar, Mr. Stevens was shocked at Gemma's total lack of interest in what to him were the most glorious languages, but he could see that her method would work. Even reading back parrotlike what she had written down, she made very few mistakes. He could imagine—distressing though it was to think about—that by the time of the performances Gemma would sound almost as proficient as Lady Jane had really been.

"I can only hope," he told Miss Jenkins, "my sixth form won't get on to the fact that you can sound wonderfully competent without even a smattering of knowledge."

It was therefore no surprise to him that though Gemma was not quite as interested as she had been at her previous coachings, she still, in what he considered her extraordinary way tackling her problem, did better than most of the pupils he had coached. At the end of their half hour he questioned her. "You seem to learn by heart extraordinarily quickly. I can't understand why you are not in a higher stream."

Gemma was putting her exercise book in which her phonetic Latin and Greek was written away in her bag. She paused, wondering how best to explain. "I'm no earthly good at the sort of lessons that count—like mathematics."

"I'm sure you could do well if you worked."

"Not really. My mother was no good either. Do you know, she still counts on her fingers?"

"Did you work out this means of mastering a foreign language for yourself?"

Gemma spoke carefully. Whatever happened, she must not mention films. "I acted in plays, and in one, as I told you, I had to speak Chinese. That's awfully difficult, but I learned the words this way, and when I had the sounds sort of right, I went over and over them with my Chinese coach to make it into sense."

"What play was this?"

That stumped Gemma. The film, which had been a war story in

68

which she got separated from her parents when the Japanese attacked and so had been brought up by her Chinese nurse, had been a success. The chances were Mr. Stevens would have heard of it.

"I . . ." She hesitated. "I don't remember. I knew only my part."

This child is prevaricating, thought Mr. Stevens. *She has something to hide. I wonder what?*

Out loud he said: "That'll be all for today. I hope your cousin gets on all right."

Later that day he ran into Miss Jenkins. "Gemma is going to get through those Latin and Greek sentences with flying colors. I have a feeling she is keeping something from us."

"What sort of thing?"

"I don't know. I just know that she's not like any other pupil I have taught. In some ways, young as she is, I feel she has great experience. I can't put it nearer than that."

"I'm awfully glad she can learn the Latin and Greek scenes," said Miss Jenkins. "I don't know whom else I could trust with the part of Lady Jane."

After about a week of lying quietly in bed, taking little interest in anything, Lydia suddenly recovered.

"I'm hungry," she told the nurses who were making her bed.

After that she got stronger rapidly. Her head got quite well, and so did her various bruises and cuts. That left just her leg, which was in a sling.

"She's very dancing-minded," Alice said. "She's certain to ask soon when she can dance again. What am I to tell her?"

The doctor avoided a direct answer. "There's a long way to go before we shall know the answer to that. When we let her out of hospital, she will not be able to put the injured leg to the ground for at least two months."

Alice shivered. "Lydie mustn't know that. I suppose we must let the bad news come to her gradually."

"I think if she asks, we shall have to let the child know she is leaving here on crutches," the nurse said. "After all, she will be eleven in April—too old to be fobbed off with fairy tales."

Alice could feel that neither the doctor nor the nurse was absolutely certain that Lydia's hip would get perfectly well, but she could not face asking outright.

"I'll get my husband to tell Lydie about the crutches," she said. "He was second leader of the fiddles with the Steen. He had to give it up because of his hands, so he's used to bad news."

"Good," said the doctor, "you do that, and if I'm about, I'll have a talk with him. Now don't worry, Mrs. Robinson, it won't help you or Lydie."

Philip saw Lydia that evening. She took the news about the crutches quite casually. She counted on her fingers.

"Two months is eight weeks. That means my hip will be well again by the end of January or the beginning of February. That's okay because I'll be ready for Gemma and Sisters at Easter."

Philip was glad she accepted the news so calmly, but he had a sinking feeling inside. Suppose, just suppose the hip was not well again by the end of January or the beginning of February, what would Lydia say then?

When Philip had kissed Lydia good night, the nurse beckoned him into the hall.

"Come into my room a moment, Mr. Robinson. Mr. Pound, Lydie's doctor, would like a word with you."

14 ❦ A Scheme

REHEARSALS FOR LADY JANE began a week after Lydia's accident. Gemma had not much to do with the early scenes in which Jane was a child of not yet ten. Although these scenes were laid in that corner of the great hall of her home, Bradgate in Leicestershire, where the child did her lessons, many of them were between Jane's parents, her tutor, and Mrs. Ellen, her nurse.

"There was such a lot of history to explain," Miss Jenkins told Gemma, "for I do want everybody to enjoy the play, not just those who know Lady Jane's story."

Yet even in the early scenes Gemma had a lot to learn. For though Jane was not yet ten, she had been studying since she was a tot, so she could already read both Latin and Greek and could speak Spanish and Italian.

Fortunately for Gemma at the early rehearsals everybody read his or her part, so with each foreign word written phonetically she could get by. Actually she did rather more than get by, so the rest of the cast were full of admiration.

"However did you learn it, Gemma?" asked the sixth-form girl who was acting the part of Jane's mother, Lady Dorset.

Gemma took coaching for granted, for in film studios there were always people employed to help when necessary with lines. "Mr. Stevens is helping me with Latin and Greek and Miss Wilson with the modern languages."

Miss Wilson was the senior modern language teacher, so the sixth-former was much impressed. "Miss Wilson and the headmaster! You're flying high, aren't you?" Then she laughed. "I wouldn't care who coached me, but I wouldn't be you for a hundred pounds. All very well while we're reading our parts, but imagine what it will be like when you haven't got the script in your hand."

Gemma couldn't explain that she had confidence because she had been taught to speak Chinese in a film. So all she said was: "I know, I expect I'll be scared stiff."

Because of Lydia's hip, it was taken for granted that the concerts for Gemma and Sisters at Christmas would be canceled. Gemma and Ann discussed this in their bedroom.

"I must say I'm glad," Ann said. "I know Mr. Forrest said I could start singing solos again after Christmas, but if I were singing in January, I should have to practice before then, and he wouldn't like that."

"I can't tell you how glad I am they're off," Gemma said. "I have to slave just learning Lady Jane. We are supposed to be word-perfect by the beginning of next term. I don't think I could have been if we'd done Gemma and Sisters."

Robin and Nigs were the two who were upset by the thought of no concerts. They went to see Lydia after school one afternoon and discussed the situation on their way to the hospital.

"It's too miserable to be true," said Robin. "Because I should think that'll mean there'll be no more concerts until Easter, for you know what Ann's like about concerts in term time, and now Gemma's being that awful Lady Jane, she doesn't want them either."

"Who was Lady Jane?" Nigs asked.

"One of those types who wanted to be queen and had her head cut off," Robin explained. "The most sickening thing is the new song I was swirling for the girls is not only my best but there was plenty of drums for you."

"Why not get on with it for Easter?" Nigs suggested.

Robin shrugged his shoulders. "Easter's such ages away, you can't really believe it will ever come. Why, we could easily be attacked by Martians by then."

72

Nigs was not allowing Robin to change the subject from his new song to Martians. "What was the song you were doing?"

"It's called 'The Carrion Crow.' It's got four verses. The first one goes: 'A carrion crow sat on an oak, Der-ry, der-ry, der-ry, dec-co; A carrion crow sat on an oak, Watching a tailor shaping his cloak. Heigh-ho! the carrion crow, Der-ry, der-ry, der-ry, dec-co.' You drum on the der-ry bits and on the heigh-ho."

"Good," said Nigs. "You can sing me the tune again on the way back."

Lydia, who was coming home at the end of the week, had been promoted to her crutches. When Robin and Nigs arrived, she was hobbling up and down the wards on them with one leg off the ground, a terrible hazard to nurses who were carrying anything. She was delighted to see the boys, and after she had shown off her prowess on the crutches, she took them to sit on a bench outside the ward where they could talk in peace.

"How's the drumming, Nigs?"

Nigs pulled a face. "I haven't touched them since your hip was hurt. When there were concerts, I was allowed sometimes to practice them in the basement, but now the concerts must be off, Mom says there's no excuse and she's very glad there isn't."

"How mean can you get!" said Lydia. "She almost sounds as if she were glad my hip is hurt."

Robin broke in. "I was swirling a new song for him with drums twice in each verse."

"It's sickening," Lydia said. "But my hip will be okay by Easter. I absolutely know that it will."

"But that's simply ages away," Robin grumbled. "Nobody would swirl a song for something as far away as Easter."

"I like that from you, my boy," Lydia retorted. "Why, you swirled songs for years before Gemma and Sisters was thought of."

After the boys had gone and she was back in her bed, Lydia thought about Gemma and Sisters. Although Miss Arrowhead had written to say she was sorry about the accident and sent her a beautiful book full of photographs of dancers, Lydia was still angry with her. She could no longer show that she was angry by behaving badly at her classes, but perhaps there was another way.

73

Of course, Alice came to the ward to see Lydia every day, usually before she started work, but Philip as well always called in on his way home from the music school and waited to drive Alice home. That evening, when he arrived, he found Lydia in very good spirits. He supposed it was because she could come home in a few days.

"I hear you are doing splendidly on your crutches, so I hope to get you to school; you'll be bored at home doing nothing."

Lydia liked the idea of that—school on crutches would be fun—but she had another subject to discuss. "Robin and Nigs came to see me today; they simply hate there being no Gemma and Sisters after Christmas because of me."

"I hate putting the performances off," Philip said. "But we must just hope your hip is strong enough for dancing at Easter, and perhaps we can fit in the concerts we shall miss at Christmas then."

Lydia clutched her father's arm. "I've been thinking. I don't see why all those old people and concerts we went to last year have got to do without us because of me."

Philip was amazed. It was not like Lydia to be humble.

"The show would be no good without you; your dancing is a big part of it, not just your solo but your tap with Gemma.

"I was thinking just for Christmas somebody could dance instead of me, and I think I know exactly the right girl."

"Who?"

"You wouldn't know. Her name is Rosie Glesse."

"Can she sing as well as dance?"

"As much as I do she can, and though I don't think she's learned any tap, they're very rich, and her mother would let her have private lessons at that place where Gemma learns." Lydia suddenly saw Rosie learning tap in her mind's eye. "As a matter of fact, she's the sort who ought to be good at tap."

Philip hated disappointing people, especially clubs for the old. "Well, it's certainly an idea. I must think about it."

After her father had gone, Lydia lay back against her pillows looking, as a passing nurse told her, like a cat who has stolen the cream.

74

If Rosie dances in Gemma and Sisters, Lydia was thinking—*and her mother is sure to let her—what will Miss Arrowhead do then? She's certain to find out, as she did about me, and she won't know what to do, for I don't think even she will dare to tell Mrs. Glesse Rosie can't be the foxglove after promising her that she could and letting her take extra lessons so she can dance the part. I hope Miss Arrowhead finds out it was me who planned Rosie should dance in Gemma and Sisters because then she'll see she can't be mean to me without being paid back.*

In the car driving home Philip told Alice what Lydia had said. "I was rather touched. It's good of her to suggest someone take her place."

Alice was doubtful. "Almost too good to be true. I wonder what Lydie's up to."

Philip was terribly conscious that he had not told Alice what the doctor had said. After all, it was only a possibility. Why let Alice agonize if there was no need? But she must be generous to Lydia.

"I don't think you should be suspicious. This accident may have changed the child. She was disobeying us in riding on the main road, and this may be her way of atoning."

"It could be, I suppose," Alice said, "but I can't say I've seen any signs of penitence. Anyway, I'm not sure it's a good idea bringing in a substitute; it'll mean a lot of extra rehearsals, and both Gemma and Ann have enough to do already."

Philip thought about that.

"Whatever you may think, it was a generous idea of Lydie's, and honestly, a few performances won't hurt Ann and Gemma."

Alice patted the knee nearest to her. "I don't want to interfere. Suppose you write to Mrs. Glesse and see what she says. I expect the girl is dancing in Miss Arrowhead's show, in which case quite likely she'll think she has enough to do already. Shall we agree to abide by Mrs. Glesse's decision?"

Philip hated Alice to disagree with him. He took a hand off the wheel and gave hers a squeeze.

"All right. And don't let's look for flaws in the children. They're a good lot."

15 ❧ The Row

ANDREW GLESSE WAS what he called "self-made." His father had been a riveter in a shipyard and somehow had raised ten children on his wage packet. All the children had done well but none better than Andrew, who was a clever and inventive boy, so had risen from messenger in a factory to be its managing director. On his way up he had married Marion, the head buyer in the women's dress department of a large store. Andrew would have liked a big family like his own, but fate had other plans, and all he and Marion could produce was Rosie, whom they both worshiped.

It was extraordinary how nice the doted-on Rosie had remained. Andrew was a rich man, and his only daughter could practically have anything she liked. But Rosie was undemanding; indeed, she seldom asked for anything, for what she most longed for no one could buy her: It was to be as talented at dancing as her mother believed her to be.

The letter from Philip arrived when Marion was alone in the house. She read it through twice before putting it against the clock on the mantelpiece to give to Andrew when he came in. As she supervised Mrs. Crow, who did the housework, her mind kept returning to the letter, and it pleased her so much and she was so pleasant that Mrs. Crow wondered if she was ill.

Marion knew who Philip was. Andrew had subscribed when

Headstone had given him a dinner and a car when he retired from the Steen. She had never known or wished to know the Robinsons, not because they were not suitable people to know, for musicians and folk like that could know anybody, but the Robinsons were not anywhere near as rich as the Glesses, and that made it awkward when it came to entertaining. But Gemma and Sisters was something apart. She would never forget seeing that little Lydia dance and thinking how unfair it was not her Rosie. And now it could be her Rosie. Of course, it might be rather much for Rosie with her solo foxglove dance to learn; still the letter said "just January," and that wouldn't interfere too much. There wouldn't be any need to say anything to Miss Arrowhead either, no good stirring up trouble; after all, she had let Lydia dance, and what was sauce for the goose was sauce for the gander.

Marion Glesse was so cock-a-hoop about Philip's offer that she had to tell Rosie when she came home from school. She expected Rosie to be overjoyed, but annoyingly, she was nothing of the sort.

"Dance instead of Lydie! Oh, Mom, I never could. I mean, people who'd seen Lydie would think me a bit of a comedown."

"What nonsense you do talk!" Marion said. "I'm sure you dance every bit as well as Lydia and better." Then she remembered something. "Mr. Robinson says there's a tap dance to do with Gemma; she's a cousin of the Robinsons."

The tap dance cheered Rosie up a little. "I think I could learn that; even Miss Arrowhead says my footwork is neat."

"It seems they teach it up at that theatrical school, but of course, you will have private lessons."

"You will ask Miss Arrowhead if I can dance instead of Lydie, won't you?" Rosie begged. "She'll be awfully angry if she finds out you haven't asked."

Marion Glesse always swept away what she did not want to hear. "She'll be told what she will be told. Now relax, dearie, and leave everything to Dad and me to fix up. All Mom's Rosie has to do is to concentrate on her clever feet."

When Andrew came in, Marion handed him Philip's letter. "I want Rosie to do this for Gemma and Sisters. It's a smart little

77

show, but you see what the letter says: 'All the rehearsals will be held in my house.' How do we feel about that? Trelawny Drive isn't quite our style, is it?"

Andrew thought about that. Certainly Trelawny Drive was not their style, for it was in a quarter of Headstone where they never visited. Still, he did not believe in being snobbish.

"I should think it would be all right. They say Robinson is a nice chap and much missed by his fellow musicians in the Steen. So I'd say yes. After all, there's no need for Rosie to see anything of the Robinsons once the concerts are over."

Mrs. Glesse's letter agreeing to allow Rosie temporarily to take Lydia's place in Gemma and Sisters arrived two days later. The family was having breakfast, so Philip told them the news.

"Lydie had a very generous idea. She didn't want those people to whom we had promised Gemma and Sisters to be disappointed, so she suggested a substitute. Her name is Rosie Glesse. She learns dancing with Lydie, and apparently she can sing a bit. This letter is from the child's mother agreeing she may replace Lydie for January."

"Goody!" said Robin. "Me and Nigs will start practicing right away."

Gemma had been eating her breakfast in a dream. Children in Lady Jane Grey's day were frequently sent away from home to be taught and disciplined in other people's houses, just as many children are sent away to boarding schools today, she thought. Jane was sent to live with Queen Catherine Parr before she was ten. The scene Gemma was studying was her arrival at court. She found it absolutely absorbing, for there was so much she must express: the child's homesickness and terror of a strange world disguised by the dignity she had to show always because she was a royal personage. Then, into the middle of her thinking about Lady Jane floated what her uncle had said. Someone called Rosie was to replace Lydia. She turned to Philip.

"You don't mean we are going to give concerts in January after all?"

"That's what I was explaining, but it won't be too much work, nothing grand, just old people's Christmas parties and things like that."

"Grand or not," said Ann, "it'll mean practicing a song, and Mr. Forrest won't like it."

Robin's cheeks were crimson with rage. "How mean can you be! You'll be old someday, Ann, and then I'll bet you'll be glad of people like us to come and give you a concert."

Gemma felt desperate. "I simply haven't got time to teach someone new. Lady Jane is an awfully long part, and I have to be word-perfect by the beginning of next term."

"I wish they weren't letting you be Lady Jane," said Robin. "Ever since you knew you were going to act her, you've been duller and duller. You never speak to any of us now."

Philip was amused. "I'm afraid there's a grain of truth in what he says, Gemma. Cheer up. According to Lydie, her friend Rosie should be easy to teach. Her parents are arranging for private lessons in tap for her dance with you."

Gemma felt quite sick. She had forgotten the tap dance. "Oh, no! Couldn't we at least cut the tap dance? It'll take ages to learn with somebody new. I'm not much good myself; I couldn't teach somebody who doesn't know much tap either."

"I expect you'll find she'll soon pick it up." Alice comforted her. "An hour for a morning or two should be all she'll need."

An hour for a morning or two! Gemma had planned the Christmas holidays with great care. Each day after breakfast she would do the housework that she had to do; then, as soon as Ann was out of their bedroom, she would get down to Lady Jane. There would be her banjo lessons with Ted and her dancing lessons to interrupt her, but otherwise, every second of the holidays she would work on her part. Now this news. Suddenly, for the first time since she had lived with the cousins, she stopped being Gemma Robinson and became Gemma Bow—the child film star. She got up and faced the family, her chin in the air.

"You can all shout and scream as much as you like. But I am an actress, and if I want to study my part, I shall study it. All right, put

79

on Gemma and Sisters with this Rosie in Lydie's place but she won't be the only change, for you'll need someone to replace me. So there!" Then Gemma marched out of the room, slamming the door behind her.

16 ✌ Being a Family

PHILIP GAVE a lot of thought to Gemma's outburst. All day between lessons he tried to see both sides of the question. In the evening, when he picked up Alice at the hospital, his mind was clear.

"I've been thinking about Gemma all day," he told Alice.

"I wouldn't take what she said too seriously." Alice counseled him. "She's very like her mother in some ways. Rowena was always flying off the handle about something. But she was sorry afterward. I shouldn't wonder if Gemma was waiting for you now to tell you that she's sorry."

"I don't want her to be sorry," Philip said. "I want her to understand my point of view."

"Well, I must say I wouldn't mind hearing that," said Alice. "At the moment my sympathies are with Gemma. Evidently this Lady Jane is a big part, and you know what acting means to her. Since you had a real excuse to get out of the concerts because of Lydie, I must say I don't see why you wanted to put this Rosie into the concert. I told you I would abide by the Glesses' decision and I do, but I still don't see why you want to do the shows."

Philip marshaled his thoughts. He must be careful not to frighten Alice by telling her his real reason for wanting to keep Gemma and Sisters alive.

"We're a family, and we've always done things together. Of

81

course, it's natural, as the children grow up, that they each go their own way, but I want us to remain a family as long as possible. Well, Gemma and Sisters does just that. We're all involved, even you seeing to the girls' frocks."

"There was no thought of giving up Gemma and Sisters," Alice told him. "It was only while Lydie was laid up."

Philip struggled on. "I know, but only Robin cared. I mean, it suited Ann and Gemma, but as a result, a whole lot of people we had promised to entertain were to be disappointed. Only Lydie saw that and found an answer."

"I'm still puzzled about Lydie," said Alice. "I know you think it's looking for a flaw in her, but somehow such altruism is out of keeping."

Philip spoke carefully. "I think it's rather optimistic to talk about Lydie dancing at Easter. We don't know yet that she'll be able to. I mean, it's rather soon."

Alice hesitated. She longed to ask, "Are you hiding something from me? Do you know something I don't?" But she could not make herself do it. Instead, she said: "Well, let's hope for Easter. There's no harm in being optimistic."

"No harm at all"—Philip agreed—"and no harm either in praying for good news."

Alice was right: Gemma was ashamed of herself. It had taken her most of the day to feel ashamed, but she had achieved it in the end. When she was free to think, she had argued against herself. *I was right to tell Uncle Philip they could do Gemma and Sisters without me. I'm an actress, so I'm right not to want to waste my time when I should be working at Lady Jane.*" But by the time school was over the argument had thinned. *Well, I suppose I needn't have said I wouldn't be in Gemma and Sisters. I suppose Uncle Philip didn't mean to be unfair to me; he just doesn't understand. Anyway, I suppose I can make time to work with this Rosie, though goodness knows how bad the tap will be with neither of us any good at it.*

Ann, who hated rows, dreaded the walk home. The walk to school in the morning had been bad enough with Gemma raging away, but to have to go through it twice was too much. So it was like an unexpected treat when Gemma joined her looking quite cheerful.

"I shouldn't have said I wouldn't do Gemma and Sisters. Of course, I'll have to. I suppose by starting before breakfast I can manage to learn my part and rehearse Rosie as well. I shall tell Uncle Philip I'm sorry."

"I should think it'll be in the Easter holidays you'll be too busy with Lady Jane to do anything else," said Ann.

Gemma shook her head. "Not really. I suppose as it's so near the production date, we'll have some rehearsals in the holidays, but it's the beginning of the summer term when the real rush will start. Dress rehearsals and all that."

"What I can't imagine," said Ann, "is why Lydie wants this Rosie to take her place. Have you ever seen Rosie at your dancing lessons?"

"No. She's not in my class. But then, a girl who can dance a solo wouldn't be. I suppose Lydie wanted her just for niceness."

Ann thought about that.

"I suppose so, but it's so queer Rosie turning up suddenly. I mean, she's not a friend of Lydie's we've ever heard of. I'd bet it's some plan Lydie's got, though goodness knows what, but you know what she is."

Philip received Gemma's apology with relief. "I was sure you didn't mean it. If you had, we should have been up a gum tree, for we certainly couldn't get a substitute for you. It's strange this gift you've developed for producing, for you'd never done it before."

"I've watched lots of films being made."

"But that's very different from stage production."

"Yes, but Mommy acted in plays, and I often went to rehearsals. I think it's the sort of thing you pick up, and I was interested because I want to be an actress on the stage when I grow up."

Philip put an arm around her. "Which I am sure you will be. I thought, if it suits you, we'd have a rehearsal on Saturday to teach Rosie the songs and to show her how we work."

Gemma had no wish to sacrifice her Saturday, but having said she was sorry, she was not going to tell her uncle how she felt.

"That'll be okay, and Lydie's being home will help because she can show Rosie about going off to change her shoes and all that."

Philip fetched Lydia home on Saturday morning. She had a great reception. Robin, with Nigs's help, had painted "Welcome home, Lydie" on an old pillowcase, and this they rigged up over the front door. Alice was cooking Lydia's favorite lunch of roast chicken with vast quantities of stuffing, followed by meringues bursting with whipped cream. Ann had bought the invalid a little cyclamen for her dressing table, and Gemma a box of her favorite chocolates. Lydia, though she looked white and thin from six weeks in hospital, was in glorious spirits. Alice had wondered whether she would be able to get up the rather steep stairs to her attic bedroom, but she was up there within five minutes of getting home. She looked at the towel rail which she had used when she did pliés before breakfast.

"I'll soon be using that again," she told Ann, Gemma, and Robin, who had followed her up. "I bet it won't be long after I throw away the crutches before I'm dancing."

Gemma crossed her fingers. It was, she thought, frightening the way Lydia took it for granted her hip would get perfectly well.

Lydia, having admired the cyclamen, opened Gemma's box of chocolates, and they all sat on the bed, chewing.

"There's a rehearsal tonight for your Rosie," Robin told Lydia. "What's she like?"

"She's nice," said Lydia.

"Does she dance well?" Ann asked.

Lydia had to explain.

"With her feet she does, but the rest of her is stiff. She moves as if she were made of wood. But I thought she could do that doll dance I do; she learned it like we all did when she learned with Polly; you are meant to be stiff doing that."

Robin was anxious about his songs. "Can she sing all right?"

"I haven't heard her," Lydia confessed, "but she sings in her

84

school choir; she told me so. That's one reason why I chose her."

Alice came up to see how the invalid was getting on. "Oh, darlings!" she said. "Not chocolates! I've the most enormous lunch cooking."

"Chocolates never interfere with my eating chicken," Robin stated.

Alice put the lid on the box. "I believe you, but no more. I won't have my lovely lunch neglected."

Poor Rosie was very nervous when she got into the car with her father to be driven to the rehearsal at Trelawny Drive. Her father noticed this. "What you got to be nervous about? I'm sure you can knock spots off these Robinsons."

Rosie thought that too silly to be passed. "Ann sings really well, even Mom says so, and they'll know the songs; I mean, she and Gemma will. Imagine if they made me sing alone!"

"I'm sure you'll do it very nicely; after all, you're in your school choir."

"Well, I can sing in tune, and then there's my dance."

Mr. Glesse laughed. "Now don't tell me you're scared of dancing. Your Mom says you're the smartest at the dancing school."

"That's what Mom thinks," said Rosie, "but not what Miss Arrowhead thinks. Anyway, I know for myself I'll never dance like Lydie."

Mr. Glesse did not hold with humility; he liked success talk. "What nonsense! You hold that head up, and as you walk into the rehearsal say to yourself, 'I'm the tops.' You think that way, and you will be."

In any event there was nothing for Rosie to be scared about. In fact, after five minutes she found the rehearsal fun. And when her father called for her at seven o'clock, she was sorry to go home.

In the car her father looked at her glowing cheeks. "That's more like my girl. You were the tops all right. I can see that."

"I wasn't," said Rosie truthfully, "but I learned the songs all right. It must be gorgeous to be them, you know, part of a big family."

Mr. Glesse did know. "You're right there, nothing like it. Still, your Mom and I are very satisfied with our one girlie. And there's a thing to remember when you're part of a big family: You don't have the best of everything the way you do. That's a point, isn't it?"

Rosie thought of the Robinsons' little sitting room with them all gathered around the piano, laughing and teasing each other. And then she thought of her very comfortable but rather empty home.

"I suppose it is," she said doubtfully.

17 ❧ Over the Coffee Cups

GEMMA DISCOVERED that somehow without too much effort she was able to fit in all she had to do, and neither Lady Jane nor Gemma and Sisters suffered. It was nearly the end of the term, so there were now three rehearsals a week of *Lady Jane* after school hours. Saturdays were Gemma's rush days, for there was Polly's dancing class, then back home for her banjo lesson with Ted, then immediately after lunch off to the drama school for her tap lesson, home to tea and a rehearsal for Gemma and Sisters. She tried to fit in working on Lady Jane on Saturdays, but she was usually too sleepy after the rehearsal to do much good, so she had to be content with giving up her Sundays to her part.

Alternately Gemma had always been a quick and accurate study. Even when she was a small child, there was very seldom a retake in a film because it was she who fluffed her lines. In fact, Miss Jenkins congratulated her on the number of scenes she could manage without her script.

"It's not the words that I find difficult," Gemma said. "It's getting Jane right. I think and think about her, but she's not easy to understand."

"I found that when I was writing the play." Miss Jenkins agreed. "She was a complex child, so brilliant yet in some ways so humble and in others so very royal."

Lydia was a bit of an anxiety. She hated feeling she could not do everything that everybody else could do, so she did her best to ignore the fact she could use only one leg. This was all right at school, where the teachers could keep an eye on her, but at home both Philip and Alice were scared whenever they were out that she would do something silly. Alice came in one day to find her sliding down the banister. When she caught her and scolded her, Lydia said: "But it's the easiest way to come down. Crutches are so awkward on stairs."

Another day Philip met her in the drive speeding along wearing a roller skate on her good leg, propelling herself by a crutch. That time he was cross.

"For your own sake don't be so silly. What chance would you have of getting on with your dancing if you break your leg?"

"I shan't," Lydia protested. "I'm very good on one skate."

But though she did not tell anybody, she did not put the roller skate on again.

One afternoon on her way to the hospital Alice ran into Miss Arrowhead.

"How's Lydie?" Miss Arrowhead asked.

"Thank goodness she's home," Alice said. "She's on crutches and will be for some time. My husband takes her to and from school every day, so she's not too bored, but you can imagine Lydie doesn't take kindly to crutches, and she has to use them for two months."

Miss Arrowhead could see that Alice was anxious, and indeed, she was herself.

"I shall be very glad to have her back. I never stop praying she makes a complete recovery, but of course, we must be patient. An injury to a hip is a serious matter for anyone, let alone a dancer. Which reminds me of something else I wanted to speak to you about."

They were standing close to a little teashop.

"Shall we go in there and have a cup of coffee?" Alice suggested. "Luckily I'm a bit early for the hospital."

They sat down at a small table, and Alice ordered the coffee.

"I am taking it for granted," Miss Arrowhead said, "that Lydie makes a complete recovery, so I'm thinking ahead. She will be eleven in April, won't she?"

"That's right."

"That means in the ordinary way she would go to Headstone Consolidated in the autumn?"

"Of course."

"I see you haven't thought about this, but I don't see how Lydie can go to that school and keep up her dancing. By next autumn she should be having a daily class. Ideally that should be first thing in the morning; not possible, of course, so it will have to be after school. I don't see how she can have an hour's lesson with me and do all the homework the Consolidated pupils are supposed to get through."

Alice did see. Even Gemma, who had less work than Ann, came home with at least two hours' work in her bag. It would be almost impossible for Lydia to manage homework on top of an hour's dancing lesson and still have time for a little recreation before bed, something she and Phillip considered a must.

"They say at the school she's at now that Lydie's bright. That should put her in the top stream. If my eldest girl, Ann, is anything to go by, that will mean Lydie will have masses of homework and have to work really hard if she is to keep up."

"Isn't there another school she could go to?" Miss Arrowhead asked. "Something smaller that could consider the requirements of individual children?"

Alice shook her head. "There used to be both a secondary modern and the old grammar school, but we were unlucky in Headstone; they did away with the splendid old grammar and joined it to the secondary modern to make this huge comprehensive."

"And you don't like it?"

Alice made a face. "It's too big, and though Ann is doing all right, my niece, Gemma, went through a bad patch. I think these consolidated schools are very hard on the less bright children; they are apt to make them feel inferior." Alice smiled. "As it happens, it takes more than a consolidated school to keep Gemma down, but I can think of a lot of children who would be far better off in the old secondary modern."

Miss Arrowhead sipped her coffee. "If Lydie is allowed to start her dancing again at the end of February, and if she progresses well, there is a chance—but only a chance—the Royal Ballet School might take her in the autumn."

Alice looked startled. "But that's in London, isn't it?"

"Yes."

Alice shook her head. "Oh, no, I'm sure my husband wouldn't allow that. He's a very family man; he wouldn't like one of the children living away from home."

"Well, we'll forget that," said Miss Arrowhead. "In any case she probably would not have got a place, for the competition is ferocious, and she will have lost more than three months' training, and trying and not succeeding might upset her."

Alice laughed. "I doubt that. Lydie would probably say the ballet school didn't know a good dancer when they saw one." She looked at her watch. "I must go or I'll be late. But I'll tell my husband what you've said; perhaps he knows of a small school where Lydie might be allowed to do her homework during games or something of that sort. Naturally we couldn't hope to make that sort of arrangement at the Consolidated."

Alice told Philip what Miss Arrowhead had said when he called for her that evening in the car.

"I told her you wouldn't let Lydie go away to school."

"Not at eleven." Philip agreed. "We shall have to lose Ann sometime, for I hope she'll get a scholarship at the Royal College of Music later on, but that's in the future."

"There isn't a smaller school Lydie could go to instead of the Consolidated, is there?"

Philip waited to answer until he was clear of some snarled-up traffic.

"I'll find out, and I'm going to find out about another school for Gemma, too. Her mother's right: She should be moved; academically she isn't working as she should. But it's no good our worrying about a school for Lydie in the autumn until we know how soon she can dance again."

Once more Alice had a feeling Philip knew something he had not told her. It was on the tip of her tongue to ask him, but she bit it back. It was nearly Christmas; if there was something to worry about, let it wait until the festival was behind her. She was so bad at hiding her feelings, it would be too tragic if her face betrayed her and as a result she spoiled Christmas for the children.

18 ❧ The Secret

THE FAMILY HAD a splendid Christmas. Gemma's crate was full of the most exotic presents, as usual beautifully packaged. The box arrived early, and it was all the family could do to keep their fingers off the parcels, they were such exciting shapes. The most exciting was the one for Lydia which was like a very large hatbox.

Robin, having prodded it all over, said: "I think it is a hat. Something enormous to wear at garden parties."

As usual, present opening had to wait until after Christmas lunch. Then, full of turkey and plum pudding and all the dessert that goes with Christmas, the family gathered around the tree, and Philip and Alice distributed the parcels. It was the custom to hand out their presents to each other first. This year, knowing how curious everybody was, Philip held up Lydia's hatbox until the very last.

"Now here's the mystery present, Lydie. We're all waiting to see what it is."

Lydia was sitting on the stairs, her crutches beside her, her injured leg propped up on a cushion. It was a convenient place for present opening. She was so excited about her mystery present, her fingers trembled as she untied the magnificent blue satin bow. When the paper was off, inside there was a gigantic hatbox; it was sprigged with forget-me-nots. Lydia lifted the lid and then, amid oohs and aahs of admiration, brought out a tutu, a real one made of white satin with the brief skirts of tarlatan and tulle.

Lydia was so pleased, she couldn't speak. Rowena, far away in Los Angeles, would have been delighted if she could have seen the pleasure she had given. The tutu had not been her idea but a secretary's.

"Then there's Lydie," Rowena, making up her Christmas list, had said. "She ought to have something extra nice this year, for she's been hospitalized with an injured hip, and she still has to use crutches. She's the one who dances, but Gemma says she won't be doing that again until February."

"A dancer," said the secretary. "I know somebody who makes ballet dresses. I guess your niece would be tickled pink with a present like that."

Lydia was tickled pink. Holding on to the banister, she pulled herself upright and held the frock against her. "How does it look?"

Ann held the waist around Lydia's. "Perfect."

Gemma was delighted her mother had been so imaginative. "Somehow you'll have to change into it for Gemma and Sisters. It simply mustn't be wasted."

Alice turned to Philip to say that as she had always told him, Rowena could be imaginative when she wanted to, but the look on his face froze the words on her lips. He was gazing at Lydia with a heartbroken expression. She was not sure there were not tears in his eyes.

I've been a selfish beast, Alice thought. *I didn't want to hear anything frightening, so I've let him bear whatever it is alone. I'll make him tell me now, though. I won't be an ostrich any longer.*

While the family were sorting out the presents and tidying away paper and ribbon, the telephone rang. Philip went to answer it. Because the telephone was in the hall, they all could hear what was going on. First there was a pause while something was explained. Then Philip answered: "Tomorrow! Well, I don't know, it's terribly short notice. Yes, we are ready, but there's a temporary understudy in the place of Lydie, who, as you know, is on crutches. I'd have to

93

find out if Rosie Glesse—that's the understudy—is free. Okay. I'll call you back." Philip faced his family.

"That was the head of your choir school, Robin. A Darby and Joan Club are having a Boxing Day party. They were to have been entertained by a concert party, but one of them has come down with mumps, so the rest are in quarantine."

"And they want Gemma and Sisters," said Robin. "Goody! Goody! I'll ring Nigs now."

Philip stopped him. "No, you won't. I agree Nigs and his drums add greatly to the entertainment. Still, we could manage without him, but we can't without Rosie. I must phone the Glesses right away."

They gathered around the telephone. Even Gemma almost hoped Rosie was free. It would be rather exciting to do a Gemma and Sisters tomorrow. Mr. Glesse answered the telephone. Philip quickly explained what had happened.

"By chance is Rosie free?"

"I don't believe she is," Mr. Glesse answered. "I seem to think there's a party somewhere. Hold on, I'll go and ask."

After a pause Mr. Glesse was back. "There was a party, but neither the wife nor Rosie thinks it matters if she misses it. Here's Rosie to talk to you."

Rosie was excited out of her usual primness. "Oh, Mr. Robinson! Fancy tomorrow!"

"Can you manage a run-through in the morning?" Philip asked.

Rosie could. "It's absolutely made my Christmas Day. Thank you so much for telling me."

In the middle of all the excitement Gemma thought of Lydia. It was sickening for her that she couldn't take part in the show. She must feel awfully out of it. But Lydia was not upset. It had been her idea to use Rosie. The sooner Rosie was dancing in public, the sooner she'd get a chance to punish Miss Arrowhead. And she would show Miss Arrowhead the gorgeous tutu; nobody would be wearing anything as beautiful as that at her concert.

It could not be pretended that Gemma and Sisters did not suffer because Lydia could not appear at the holiday-after-Christmas-Day festivities. She brought a gaiety and sparkle to everything she did. Rosie's main quality was stolidity, but she was reliable, and the doll dance suited her perfectly. She was a wooden child by nature, so she couldn't go wrong. She was less suited in the tap dance. Lydia had enjoyed doing that so much, it had been full of gaiety, which had been infectious and caught by Gemma. Rosie was an earnest tap dancer, so Gemma, missing Lydia, was earnest, too.

But the members of the Darby and Joan Club were not critical; they thought all the children marvelous. They clapped until their old hands were sore.

Lydia had gone with the family and so had seen Gemma and Sisters as audience. Philip and Alice had been afraid that she would find being a spectator hard to take, but Lydia was in some ways good to deal with; having accepted her crutches until the end of January, she never grumbled. But that did not mean she watched with an uncritical eye. Nothing escaped her, and at supper after the show she told the family all about it. She also gave some imitations which had them all crying with laughter.

Of course, Mrs. Glesse had brought Rosie to the performance and had stayed with her, fussing about her hair and her dress until the last moment, when she had joined Alice and Lydia in the front row.

"And this is what she did," said Lydia. "She was wearing that simply awful hat—can I have the tea cozy, Mom?" Lydia put the cover for the teapot on her head. "This was her when Rosie was dancing."

Mrs. Glesse had, of course, watched Rosie daily as to a tape recorder she rehearsed her doll dance. As a result, she knew every movement and believed she followed them in her head. But that was not what happened, as sharp-eyed Lydia had noticed. With a silly, infatuated expression on her face her head, with its blue hair under a toque, had moved from side to side in time with the music, and the same thing happened when Rosie tap-danced with Gemma. Cruelly Lydia imitated her.

"And if only I could use my bad leg, I'd show you watching

Rosie, Gemma, and her and you trying to catch up with each other's feet."

"Thank goodness you can't," said Alice, mopping her eyes. "I do hope Mrs. Glesse doesn't come to the next performance, for I shall never be able to keep a straight face."

"But was the show all right?" Gemma asked.

"I thought the singing was better than when I'm there because Rosie sings better than I do," said Lydia, "but, my goodness, you did look as if you were in church, even you, Gemma, especially in the first song. You were better by the end."

"How was Rosie's dance?" Gemma wanted to know. "We saw it only back view, remember."

Lydia tried to be fair. "It wasn't bad. I mean, a doll is meant to be stiff, and she was, and even her face helps; you know, she is rather like a plain doll in the ordinary way."

"Poor little Rosie!" said Alice. "We thought you sang beautifully," Alice told Ann. "Mr. Forrest would be proud of you; they simply ate up 'Bless This House.' "

The children could have gone on all night talking about the show, but Alice shooed them off to bed.

"And no gossiping upstairs," she called out. "We've a lot more concerts in January, and I want you fresh for them."

Back in the sitting room she started to pile the plates together. Then she put them down and sat in a chair facing Philip. "I've been a coward. You are worried about Lydie, aren't you? What exactly did the doctor say?"

Philip had known that someday Alice would make herself ask that question. "A lot of it was technical, but roughly it works out to this. A dislocated hip sometimes means paralysis of the leg. The only treatment is what she had—the leg in a pulley and weights. This was to give the ligaments time to heal. Then, after a couple of months on crutches, she will be X-rayed. That is when they will know the answer."

"You mean, whether she can dance again?"

"I'm afraid it's more than that. I gather there are three possible results. The first is complete recovery. The second is partial recovery. The third would mean she is crippled."

All the color left Alice's face. In a whisper she said: "A cripple! Lydie a cripple!"

Philip took her hands.

"Don't look like that. Let's believe Lydie will make a complete recovery."

"But the end of January is weeks away. Such a time to wait for news."

"I know." Philip pulled her to her feet. "A long time to wait, during which not by a flicker of an eyelash must the children know there is anything to fear. We must behave normally, and as a start, I'll help you wash up."

Alice managed something approaching a smile. "Right. Oh, dear, I do hope I can be brave. If I show a sign I am worrying, you will tell me, won't you?"

19 ❦ Tea at the Studio

ALTHOUGH SHE DIDN'T complain, the Christmas holidays dragged for Lydia. They all did what they could to help, but they were so busy with their own things they could find little time. The music school was closed, so Ann did not have her lessons with Mr. Forrest, but there were the usual choir practices and her songs to rehearse for Gemma and Sisters. Robin was often at home, but he spent his time at the piano swirling new songs, often helped out by Nigs, who now kept his drums in Robin's bedroom; that Alice found most inconvenient.

"It's such small room," she told Philip. "I fall over them each time I go in. But I suppose until the end of the holidays I must bear with them."

Philip could see how awkward drums were in a bedroom. "It would be wonderful if only the Gamesomes had a piano; they've a much bigger house than we have; then Robin could go to Nigs's for his composing. Still, I suppose we should be grateful he's happily employed for hours on end."

Gemma had no time for Lydia or anyone else. Apart from her banjo lessons and working at Lady Jane, Mrs. Glesse had arranged she should share Rosie's private tap classes. "They'll do you good, dear," she told Gemma. "I think there are moments when your timing could be improved. I thought at the last concert you were not quite in rhythm with Rosie."

"What a sauce!" said Ann when she heard. "I wonder you didn't tell her it was Rosie who wasn't keeping time with you."

Gemma laughed. "I couldn't. It's true. In her sort of way Rosie's good at tap, much better than I'll ever be. I think next autumn, unless there's a new play or anything, I shall ask Mommy if I can have private lessons and let Lydie share them; she'd be marvelous if she had proper lessons."

Of course, Gemma and Sisters was not the only excitement in the Christmas holidays. There were parties which Lydia went to, but all too often it was mostly as a spectator, for parties for children of around ten don't often include much sitting down.

"Well, I like the tea," Lydia told Alice philosophically. "And I like the crackers, and it's better than just sitting at home. But I do find this is a long January. I think every day I loathe my crutches more."

Alice took a deep breath before she could answer in a calm voice. "I'm sure you do, darling, but you've been very good about them."

There were two visits to the theater which were specially arranged for Lydia, though the whole family went. The first was to *Alice in Wonderland*, which Robin found a terrible bore. "All talk. I like things to happen."

The other was to the pantomime, and that was a great success with everybody, for it had something in it for them all. Robin fell off his seat in the kitchen scene where a pie was made in which rabbit was cooked whole in it—fur and all. There was a children's ballet, which made Lydia's day; There was so much to criticize. For Ann the principal girl had a really lovely singing voice, and Gemma was always happy in a theater. Still, two theaters, a few parties, and watching Gemma and Sisters left a lot of time on Lydia's hands. Then one day after rehearsal Rosie gave her an idea.

"I still go to my private lessons with Polly," she confided. "I feel awful not telling her about the doll dance, but Mom won't let me. I've told her and told her she ought to ask Miss Arrowhead, but she won't."

99

"I expect Miss Arrowhead's away," said Lydia. "She sometimes takes a holiday now."

Rosie shook her head. "Not this year she isn't. Girls come to rehearsals all the time. Not so much for the solos but for the ballets that use all the big girls."

Lydia brooded on this piece of news. She had been hoping for a way to see Miss Arrowhead, but she had never thought there might be rehearsals going on. If only she might go and watch rehearsals, she wouldn't be bored anymore, and somehow she'd find a way to tell her about Rosie and that it was she who had arranged it. It never crossed Lydia's mind she might be hurting Rosie. Miss Arrowhead would not be able to do anything about her; Mrs. Glesse was paying for private lessons and had already ordered the tutu and silk tights; even Miss Arrowhead wouldn't dare say Rosie couldn't dance. Once Miss Arrowhead knew that, she would see how mean she had been to her; even now she might change the ballet and find a part for her.

Looking as though she had never schemed in her life, Lydia went to her father.

"Miss Arrowhead is having rehearsals at the studio; would you telephone and ask if I could come and watch? She'll see how dull it is for me with nothing to do, and you'd take me, Dad, wouldn't you, and fetch me home?"

Philip had been thinking it was time Miss Arrowhead was taken into their confidence. If the news was bad after the X ray, they might be glad of her help in turning Lydia's attention to other careers than dancing, for Lydia had a great admiration for Miss Arrowhead. So instead of telephoning, he went to call. Miss Arrowhead had just come into the studio for her first rehearsal. She offered Philip a seat.

"How's Lydie?"

Philip explained about the rehearsals. "It would give her great pleasure if she was allowed to watch."

"Of course, she can, bless her. I'll have a comfortable chair brought in, and a stool. When's the X ray?"

"About the first week in February, I think. Do you know about injured hips?"

Miss Arrowhead nodded. "When I was training, the most brilliant pupil at the dancing school dislocated her hip."

"What happened?"

"It didn't recover. She was left, poor child, with a deformed and painful hip."

Philip took time before he answered. "Then you know the doctors can never tell if such a catastrophe has occurred until between twelve to sixteen weeks after the accident, when it will show on an X ray."

Miss Arrowhead looked at Philip, sympathy staring out of her eyes. "I know. Has Lydie any idea what could happen?"

"None."

Miss Arrowhead felt there was nothing more she could say. She got up and led the way to the door. "If you can get Lydie here this afternoon, there is rehearsal she might enjoy. Don't bother about getting her home; my niece, Polly, or I will see to that."

"Thank you. It's very good of you."

Miss Arrowhead would have liked to have laid a sympathizing hand on Philip's arm, but she restrained herself and instead said: "It's very little any of us can do except pray and never lose faith."

Lydia was charmed to hear she was to be taken to watch a rehearsal and more pleased when she saw the arrangements made for her at the studio: the comfortable armchair from Miss Arrowhead's own sitting room and the stool for her bad leg. She enjoyed the fuss made of her as well, all the big girls, many of whom she had never spoken to before, gathering around and asking her how she was. She felt like a queen, and it was very cheering up.

"We are going to rehearse the opening scene in the woods, Lydie," Miss Arrowhead explained. "These are the wood fairies; the music is some that Mendelssohn wrote for A *Midsummer Night's Dream.*"

Lydia spent an enchanted afternoon. The dance was not difficult, but few of the girls had much talent, so she was nearly always ahead of Miss Arrowhead in picking out—mentally—faults of position, footwork, and arms. It came as a shock to her when Miss Arrowhead said: "Class dismissed."

Then she came to sit down beside Lydia. "What about some tea? It's dry work watching other people dance, especially when you dance every step in your head, as I'm sure you did."

Miss Arrowhead provided a very nice tea with cheese sandwiches, of which Lydia was particularly fond. But hungry as she was, she did not forget why she was there.

"My aunt Rowena—she's our cousin Gemma's mother—gave me a simply gorgeous tutu for Christmas. She sent it from America."

Miss Arrowhead looked at Lydia's glowing face, and her heart sank. "How exciting!" And there she stopped. What on earth more was there to say? It would be cruel to promise an occasion when the child could wear it.

Lydia said: "Did you know they are doing Gemma and Sisters without me?"

"No. How are they managing?"

"Rosie Glesse is being me. I suggested her."

"Rosie! What solo dance is Rosie doing? Naughty child, she should have spoken to me."

"That doll dance. Actually she does it all right. I suggested she should dance that."

Miss Arrowhead saw Lydia's face was flushed and her eyes were overbright. Clearly allowing Rosie to take her place meant a great deal, but why? Then she guessed. "Did you think I would treat Rosie as I treated you?"

Lydia shook her head. "No, I didn't. If I had, I wouldn't have told you, because I like Rosie. I knew you wouldn't say she couldn't be the foxglove because the tutu is ordered and so are the tights and her mother has paid for private lessons."

Miss Arrowhead let all this sink in. Then she said: "You are still angry with me, aren't you?"

"Well, it was mean. Everybody dancing in your show except me. How would you have felt if you were me?"

Miss Arrowhead felt as if she had been nudged. Nobody could tell yet if, supposing Lydia could not dance, she could teach, but it certainly was a chance to show that it was possible to replan your life if things went wrong.

"I know how I should have felt, for once I was very like you and I was considered just as promising."

"And did everybody in the school dance in a ballet except you?"

"No, at my school we had regular public performances, and we all danced. I usually had a star part."

"Lucky you!" said Lydia. "So you can imagine how I feel."

Miss Arrowhead went on with her story. "In those days there was a great Russian ballet which was based in France but came over and danced in England. The man to whom it belonged came to my school and watched us dance. Afterward he sent for me and told me he would see me again in a year's time. If I continued to improve, he would take me into his ballet and make me a big star."

"Goodness!" Lydia gasped. "How gorgeous! And did he see you the next year?"

Miss Arrowhead shook her head. "Yes, but he didn't see me dance. You see, I'd grown a great deal in the year, so all he said was 'I am sorry, my child. I have no room for a beanpole; you will not make a professional dancer.' "

"How awful," said Lydia.

"It did seem so at the time," Miss Arrowhead said. "It seemed the end of the world, but it wasn't, you know; it never is. I'm very happy with my life as it is. But you see, I do understand about disappointment."

"I think leaving me out of the ballet was more than a disappointment," said Lydia. "I think it was mean."

Miss Arrowhead passed Lydia the last cheese sandwich.

"As a matter of fact, before your accident, I had thought it was a little hard, and I had planned a dance for you."

Lydia almost got out of her chair.

"No! What am I going to be? Can I wear my tutu?"

Too late Miss Arrowhead realized she should have kept quiet. "I'm afraid there's no chance of your being ready to dance a solo by the summer. You and I will have at least fourteen weeks of lessons to make up. Now I must drive you home."

Lydia picked up her crutches. "And you won't punish Rosie, will you?"

Miss Arrowhead helped Lydia on to her good leg. "Not a word, but I think, if you think about it, you'll find out it wasn't very nice of you to have told me."

But Lydia wasn't having that. "And it wasn't very nice of you not to let me dance. But I don't mind anymore now I know there's a part for me. And you wait and see, I'll be able to dance this summer, I know I will, and I'll wear my tutu."

20 ✢ Ask Polly

FROM THE POINT of view of Robin, Nigs, and Rosie all too soon the
Christmas holidays came to an end, which meant the end of the
performances of Gemma and Sisters. To everybody's surprise, in
spite of Rosie's replacing Lydia, the fame of Gemma and Sisters
had grown, and requests for performances at Easter were already
coming in.

"I've enjoyed doing the shows," Ann confided to Gemma on the
night of the last concert, "but I'm glad it's over. I know Mr.
Forrest, though he knows I've been singing, won't like the songs I
sing. He calls those sort of songs pulp, but it's what the audience likes."

"What would he like?"

"Oh, you know, 'Cherry Ripe' and that sort of thing."

"Oh, well," Gemma said comfortingly, "it's a long time to
Easter, and in the meantime, you can sing all his sort of songs."

"I tell you something we've forgotten," Ann told her, "that
concert we promised House Captain to buy a dog for the blind."

Gemma was horrified. "We couldn't do a whole concert all by
ourselves."

"We'd have to get some other people to help, perhaps the school
choir and I had thought the drama group."

"Don't be silly!" Gemma interrupted. "The drama group is
much too busy with Lady Jane to do anything else."

105

"Well, we did promise House Captain," said Ann persistently.

"You did, I didn't. You know I don't care about house marks."

"I know you don't," Ann said. "But you ought to care because if you're good as Lady Jane, you'll get a lot. I suppose we could put off the guide dog concert until Christmas, but that's such ages away; besides, I thought, if Lydie's hip is okay by Easter, as she isn't dancing in Miss Arrowhead's concert, she could do a special solo. It would give her a chance to wear the tutu your mother gave her and make up a bit for missing all the concerts this holiday."

Gemma felt terribly mean. If there were one thing that would please Lydia, it would be to wear her tutu, and if Miss Arrowhead agreed, it would be a good opportunity. But how on earth was she to squeeze in a special Gemma and Sisters at Easter? It would mean probably giving two shows, one in each half of the program, with all the extra songs and dances to learn. She knew the cousins were sick of hearing about Lady Jane, so she tried another line of argument. "We can hardly fix a concert until we know Lydie's all right to dance."

Ann was getting into bed. "Why shouldn't she be? Easter isn't until April, and she can use her leg again most likely this month."

"Well, I suppose there'll be exercises and things. I mean, from the end of January to the middle of April isn't all that far away."

"You don't want to do the concert because of Lady Jane," said Ann. "But I did promise the guide dog concert. By Christmas there'll be a new house captain. Eunice, the one we've got now, will have left."

Gemma felt desperate. It was so true about Lady Jane, but she didn't want to be mean, and of course, if the house captain was leaving, Ann, who was so crazy about winning the House Cup, would want to do the concert before she left.

"Couldn't we do it in the summer holidays?" she suggested, knowing, even as she spoke, it was a silly idea.

"And who would come?" Ann asked. "You know everybody will be away." Then Ann had an idea. "I tell you what, when you go to your dancing class on Saturday, you ask if Lydie is certain to dance

106

by Easter; people like that Polly who teaches you are sure to know. All dancing teachers must know about legs."

Worriedly Gemma climbed into bed. *Oh, dear!* she thought. *I suppose I could do that, but I know already what Polly will say. It will be yes and that will mean the guide dog concert is on. I simply can't bear it.* But out loud she said: "All right, I'll ask."

The next Saturday was the usual rush. Gemma had woken early to study her first scenes in *Lady Jane*, for rehearsals were starting on Monday. Then, after breakfast, having helped clear away and made her bed and given the bedroom a rough tidying, for it was her day, she snatched up her shoes and raced off to her dancing class.

The class Gemma attended was a large one made up of all those girls who were not up to Miss Arrowhead's standard. Polly did not find most of the children interesting to teach, but she had a warm corner in her heart for Gemma because she was outstanding at mime. So when after the class Gemma came up to speak to her, though it was only a few minutes before her next class, she gave her a welcoming smile. She had heard about Lady Jane and guessed that perhaps Gemma had to dance a pavane or whatever they danced at that date and needed help.

"Yes, dear?"

"My cousin Ann asked me to ask you if Lydie will be okay to dance at Easter."

Polly had heard from Miss Arrowhead about her conversation with Philip. She knew how terribly anxious not only the parents but Miss Arrowhead were. She knew Lydia's chances of a complete recovery were not very high, and she also knew that Lydia and, presumably, none of the children had any idea there was anything to worry about. Had she expected Gemma's question, she would have managed not to show a sign of what she knew, but she was not expecting it. As a result, Gemma, used from babyhood to studying expressions, thought Polly said rather too quickly, "I imagine so," and read something in her eyes. Scared, she gazed at her.

"You don't think that she will?"

Polly tried harder. "Honestly, dear, I know nothing about it. I don't teach Lydie. Why don't you ask your uncle and aunt?"

107

Gemma was still staring up at Polly. She could tell when people did not mean what they were saying.

"You know something, don't you? Is there something awful the matter with Lydie's hip?"

Polly was vowed to secrecy, but Gemma had to be answered. "I know only that all dislocated hips give anxiety, especially to dancers."

Gemma knew that this at least was the truth. "So nobody knows if Lydie will dance again until after the X ray?"

Polly hated herself for prevaricating, but she had to. "I expect the doctor has a pretty good idea how she's going, and I'm sure there's no need to worry."

Gemma could sense that this was not true, but she also knew that Polly would say no more.

"Thank you," she said. "I must go now."

Talking to Polly had made Gemma a little late for her banjo lesson, so she ran most of the way home. It was a stumbling sort of run, for her eyes kept filling with tears. It was not in Gemma's nature to accept quietly; she had to dramatize, with the result that before she reached Trelawny Drive, she had in her mind placed Lydia permanently in a wheelchair.

Ted Smith arrived two minutes after Gemma. He had come to a decision. He had accepted that he would have to fight to get Gemma to work at the banjo this term, for he would have to compete for every minute against Lady Jane. So he had a scheme. He told her about it right away. "I'm sick of that lady who loved a swine, and so I reckon are a good many other people, so as from today both the lady and the swine are out. In their place how would you fancy this?" He took her banjo and began to sing.

> I saw three ships come sailing by,
> Sailing by, sailing by,
> I saw three ships come sailing by,
> On New Year's Day in the morning.

Ted was just going to sing the second verse when he heard a sniff and saw that Gemma was crying. He put down the banjo.

"What's up, mate? I've heard a lot said about my voice, but no one ever cried about it before."

Gemma spoke on almost a howl. "Oh, Ted! Oh, Ted!"

"Now, now," said Ted. "Whatever it is it isn't worth that noise. Come, cough it up. What's the trouble?"

Interrupted by tearful hiccups, Gemma told him what she had heard and guessed from her talk with Polly.

"Imagine!" she sobbed. "Perhaps she'll never walk again, and she's a dancer. I think if I couldn't act, I'd just die."

Ted shut the door.

"Now you quiet down," he said firmly. "Polly didn't say anything about Lydie not being able to walk again. But from what she did say I reckon it's a worrying time for Mr. and Mrs. Robinson, and you want to help, not hinder."

"Of course. What can I do?"

"Well, you can stop crying for one thing, and you can do what your uncle and aunt are doing—put a good face on things. And I wouldn't take what Polly said or didn't say for gospel. I'd ask right out. Not when the other kids are around, of course, but when you get a chance. It's always better to know the whole truth than just the half of it. And now we'll do what I'm here for. Now here's the fingering for the new song; the words are dead easy."

That evening Gemma found Philip alone. He had just come in and was reading his letters. She shut the door and faced him. "Ann wants to do a special Gemma and Sisters to buy a dog for a blind person; we'll get house marks for it. Well, I didn't want to, and anyway, I said we didn't know for certain whether Lydie could dance by Easter, so she asked me to ask Polly. Polly wouldn't say anything except that I should ask you, but I could see in her face she didn't think—" Gemma swallowed a sob.

"Didn't think what?"

"That she would get well ever."

Philip paused for a moment; then he laid his hands on Gemma's shoulders. "You've got that wrong. Neither Polly nor anybody else thinks that. Nobody knows anything until Lydie is X-rayed. But

Aunt Alice and I have faith, strong faith that the news will be good and Lydie will make a perfect recovery."

"But if she doesn't?"

"Don't say that, and don't think it. I hadn't meant you children to know, but now you do, you've got to do the best acting you've ever done, for not by a look must Lydie or the others suspect there is anything to worry about. Can you do that?"

Gemma couldn't imagine how he could be so brave, but if he could, she could. She gave a little nod. "Yes. Nobody shall know."

21 ∽ Acting

GEMMA MIGHT NOT have been successful in keeping the fact that something was bothering her a secret from Ann if it had not been for Lady Jane. From the following Monday there were long rehearsals after school twice a week and shorter rehearsals on the other days, and Gemma found them enthralling.

In a big consolidated school there was a lot of talent, especially among the older members of the drama group. These were mostly fifth- and sixth-formers who were working so hard in school that they had to be really keen to take time off to rehearse and resented a wasted second. Not only did the actors attend rehearsals, but would-be stage managers and assistant stage managers were also there, carefully making notes as if it were a professional production. The art people came in as well, for they would have to design such scenery as was possible in the school hall and the costumes, which would be made in the dressmaking classes. Later on Gemma learned those pupils keen on lighting would also attend rehearsals, for they had good stage lighting at Headstone Consolidated. In fact, though Gemma didn't think about it in that way, she was the centerpiece of an all-out school effort. How thankful she was that she was a good study and had worked whenever it was possible at Jane all through the holidays, so that she was more or less word-perfect in all the early scenes by the time the term began.

In the first week of the term Miss Smith had a talk with Gemma about homework. "I realize that you are going to have an hour's rehearsal most days and longer on two days. This means I must reduce your work. So for this term I shall not expect you to do your English and history homework. This should give you plenty of time for mathematics and other subjects in which you are not so well up."

Gemma could see this was generous but at the same time depressing. "It's no good pretending that math is my favorite subject. I'd much rather give the time to English."

Miss Smith laughed. "I'm afraid you aren't going to be asked. Because you are acting the part of Lady Jane, I have worked out a timetable to help you, but I can't let you pick your own subjects."

Gemma thought back to Miss Court. Dear Miss Court, so unvalued at the time! There she would sit, dewy-eyed, gazing at what she considered her little genius pupil, saying: "What is really important, Gemma, is that you give everything that is in you to this part. So I think, while you are working so hard, we'll drop these tiresome sums, shall we?" However, it was no good hoping Miss Smith would suddenly become a Miss Court, so Gemma said, in what she hoped was a grateful voice: "It's awfully kind of you. I'll try to improve my math."

Gemma discovered she did not have to struggle to make Ann listen to her descriptions of rehearsals, for Ann was thrilled to hear about them. To her all seniors had the mystic quality of gods and goddesses, and any words dropped about them were received with devotion. She particularly could not hear enough about the head of Gemma's house, Eunice, who was playing one of Jane's ladies.

"What's she like? Has she said what house marks you'll get?"

With all the seniors with whom she worked Gemma seldom exchanged a word except about the play, but Eunice had said something personal, and she had treasured this for Ann.

"She didn't say anything about house marks, but there is a scene where I hear I have to leave home and go to the court, and when we rehearsed that the first time, she said: 'You know, Gemma Robinson, you are going to be all right in this part.'"

112

Ann was knocked breathless at praise from such a source.

"Oh, Gemma! How glorious for you! What did you say to her?"

Gemma did not think Eunice was qualified to judge acting when she saw it. She was good casting for the lady as she had a sort of matter-of-fact gruffness which fitted the role, but she was not telling Ann that.

"I just said 'thank you,' but I shouldn't fuss. I'm certain I'll get some house marks."

"If it had been me"—Ann sighed—"I should have felt like Alice in Wonderland: 'Curtsy while you're thinking what to say. It saves time.' "

It was curious, Gemma found, how impossible it was to make outsiders see the drama group's rehearsals as they were. In most other school things there were the usual giggling and whisperings and larking about, but not at drama rehearsals. They were all hard work, and anyone who didn't work could get out. This, by Gemma's standards, was exactly what rehearsals ought to be. She had learned in a hard school. Time was money in film studios, so any fooling about was more than frowned upon. That those who produced her and the seniors who worked with her found this dedicated attitude strange in a child of her age never crossed her mind. But they did find it strange and outside rehearsals spoke of Gemma not only to each other but to Mr. Weldon, who taught senior English and who was producing *Lady Jane*, and to Miss Jenkins.

"Don't you think she's going to be extraordinarily good?"

"You wouldn't think she was only thirteen, would you?"

"When I'm acting with her, I forget she's Gemma Robinson and treat her as Lady Jane."

"Better watch out," Mr. Weldon said, "for the scenes when she's queen or you'll find yourselves treating her like one off as well as on."

Of course, news of how good Gemma was going to be was not confined to the cast; it filtered through the school until it reached Ann.

"I hear your cousin is going to be a smashing Lady Jane."

113

"Someone said if your cousin Gemma couldn't be Lady Jane, Miss Jenkins wouldn't do the play."

Ann longed to tell them who Gemma was. It seemed dishonest somehow to pretend she was an inexperienced schoolgirl, but of course, she couldn't say a word. Nor did she tell Gemma what was being said. Gemma, to her mind, had quite a good enough opinion of herself as it was; she didn't need any bucking up.

In the second week after rehearsals had started, there was news for Lydia. Alice and Philip came home early to find the children finishing tea.

"You are to be X-rayed on Monday," Alice said.

Lydia went on eating. "Goody! I'm sick of these old crutches."

Philip, passing her chair, rubbed Lydia's curls the wrong way. "You won't be able to throw them away at once. You're bound to have remedial exercises, it's so long since you used that leg."

"I can't do remedial exercises too long," said Lydia. "I've missed fifteen weeks of dancing lessons, so I've got to work like a slave to catch up so I can dance in Miss Arrowhead's public performance in my tutu."

Gemma gave a quick look at Philip and Alice. There was nothing on their faces to show how anxious they were. For fear her own face was less controlled she looked down, pretending to brush some crumbs from her lap. *How strange that they can behave like that*, she thought. *In a way it's acting—good acting—yet they can't act. I just don't understand. Oh, goodness! I wish Monday were tomorrow. Imagine, a whole weekend to wait!*

22 ❦ The X Ray

OF COURSE, the weekend did pass—it always does. Saturday was as usual a busy day for Gemma, and on Sunday after church she set herself down to go over and over the two difficult scenes in one of which she spoke Latin and in the other Greek. Though she had learned all the speeches phonetically, she knew what the words meant, and now she had to get them to run off her tongue as though she thought in both languages. She worked in the bedroom as Ann was out singing in the choir, only breaking off to come down to tea, and she was still working when Ann came home from evensong.

"Listen, Ann," said Gemma, and ran off one of the speeches. "Does this sound as though I know Greek?"

Gemma knew that she said the speech well, and she expected a little admiration from Ann, so she was surprised when she was answered with a sniff. The sniff was followed by a hiccup, and it was then Gemma realized Ann was crying. Ann, who never cried! Gemma, who had been sitting on her bed, jumped up and ran to Ann and tried to put her arms around her, but she was pushed away.

"Don't be nice to me. I mustn't cry, not now, for we've got to go down to supper and nobody must see."

"But what's up? What's happened?"

115

Ann fought for composure. "It's something you don't know anything about."

"How do you know I don't if you don't tell me?" Gemma asked.

Ann was getting control of herself. "I suppose it won't matter telling you now. Everybody will know tomorrow."

Gemma gave a gasp. "Do you mean about Lydie?"

Ann was sitting at the dressing table. She swung around. "I didn't know you knew. Who told you? Was it Polly?"

Gemma thought. "Not exactly, but it was what she wouldn't say. Then I asked Uncle Philip. How did you find out?"

"It was Polly really," Ann explained. "When you'd seen Polly, as you said you would, I asked you if she knew when Lydie could dance again and you said that she didn't know because she didn't teach Lydie. Well, I thought about that, and it seemed odd somehow—I mean, if she'd said she knew nothing about dislocated hips, it would have made sense, but not just because she didn't teach Lydie. Then you were so odd. I mean, you'd gone to ask because of that concert for the dog for the blind, and suddenly you wouldn't talk about it anymore, you shut up like a closed door, so I thought *something's* wrong. Then I found out."

"How?"

"Well, you know Audrey in my class. Well, her dad's a doctor. I vowed her not to say why she wanted to know but to ask her father about dislocated hips. Luckily he's the sort of father who answers questions without wanting to know why."

"And what did he say?" Gemma asked.

"Audrey wrote it down for me." Ann opened a drawer and brought out a handkerchief sachet she had been given for Christmas. Out of it she took a paper from an exercise book. " 'A dislocation of the hip,' " she read, " 'may be accompanied by total paralysis of the leg,' or a dislocated hip joint may lose its blood supply, in which case it will collapse.' Audrey's father said, 'Doctors can never be certain what has happened until after an X ray.' "

Gemma watched Ann put away the piece of paper in the sachet. "Why didn't you say anything? I mean, you could have told Uncle Philip and Aunt Alice that you knew."

Ann put the sachet back in the drawer. "I wouldn't talk about it. It's too awful. I wouldn't now, only you saw me crying. It was a hymn in church started me off. I nearly cried right there in the choir stall. Imagine!"

"What was the hymn?"

"That one that begins 'At even ere the sun was set, The sick, O Lord, around thee lay.' I knew we were singing it, of course, as we'd been through it at choir practice, but I suppose, because it's tomorrow they X-ray Lydie, I suddenly thought: Suppose Lydie is like that, lying around, asking for help."

Gemma gripped Ann's arm. "You mustn't think that. Uncle Philip said that he and Aunt Alice never think like that. They've got faith, he told me, that Lydie's going to be perfectly okay."

"Did they?" Ann looked up at Gemma, longing to believe. "As a matter of fact, Audrey's father did say sometimes dislocated hips get perfectly well but not often."

Robin came halfway up the stairs, shouting as he came: "Supper, you two, and it's sausage and potatoes, so you'd better hurry."

"Oh, goodness! Do I look as if I'd been crying?" Ann asked.

Gemma could truthfully say the tears didn't show, but as she walked downstairs behind Ann, she had a new respect for her. Somehow she'd thought her rather a cold fish, but there she'd been with all this bottled up inside her, never saying a word.

Now that school had started again, there were no afternoon rehearsals for Miss Arrowhead's ballet. Instead, rehearsals started after school, and whenever she could get a lift, Lydia was there to watch. On the Monday afternoon after her X ray Philip delivered her as usual. It was by now established that Polly drove her home. When Lydia clattered in on her crutches, Miss Arrowhead came to meet her. She tried to sound casual. "Still got your crutches?"

Lydia lowered herself into her chair. "As soon as they've seen the X ray, I can start exercises, and I won't need them after that. Perhaps just a stick till the leg I haven't used is strong, but I shouldn't think I'd want that more than two days."

"When will you know the result of the X ray?"

"Ordinarily it might take up to a week, but Mom says there are perks from working in a hospital; she thinks she'll get a squint at it long before then."

Miss Arrowhead asked no more questions, sure that when there was any news—good or bad—someone would let her know.

"I'm rehearsing the soloists this afternoon. You must be a good girl and not make them feel shy."

"I won't. Is Rosie coming?"

"Yes."

"I think," said Lydia. "very odd flowers grow in your wood, but I suppose they do in ballets."

"You mustn't call this a ballet, Lydie. A ballet—at least a modern one—is something planned by a choreographer to tell a story or show a pattern in terms of dancing, and what that sort of ballet needs is good dancers, nobody trying to shine but all being part of the story or design."

"I wouldn't like that," said Lydia firmly. "When I dance in a ballet, I want to shine more than anybody else."

Miss Arrowhead looked at Lydia, so small and fair and determined, sitting in the big chair, her crutches beside her. *Oh, darling,* she thought, *if, pray God, you can dance again, you will shine, I'm sure you will.* To Lydia she said: "Someday I hope you will see some modern ballets, and then you will understand what I'm talking about."

That evening Philip got home long before Alice. He found Robin at the piano, trying to swirl something which sounded very like church music against a background of Lydia's telling him about Miss Arrowhead's ballet.

"Well, when the rabbits have gone off—very bad they are, all hopping at different times—the flowers come alive," she was saying, "I think they're odd sort of flowers, I mean, there aren't any primroses or celandines but grand flowers like a wild rose, a bluebell, and a foxglove, that's Rosie. My goodness, I wish I could show you Rosie being a foxglove!"

"Mom's going to be late," said Philip. "She said to see the fish pie was in the oven."

Robin struck a chord. "It is. Ann put it in after tea."

Philip looked at the table.

"Whose day is it to lay up?"

Robin closed the piano. "I was afraid you were going to ask that—it's mine."

Philip went to the bottom of the stairs and called to Ann. She came out of her room and hung over the banister.

"Mom will be late home," Philip explained. "She said we weren't to wait. Does the gas need turning up on the fish pie?"

Ann ran down the stairs. "What about the X ray? Lydia doesn't seem to know anything."

"Nor do we, but your mother seems very in with the X ray department, so she hopes for some early news—it can take several days, you know."

Ann slipped her arm through her father's. She wished she were good at saying nice things, but she wasn't, so all she managed was: "Gemma's just home from her rehearsal, and the pie should be hot, so we may as well have supper right away—I expect you're hungry."

The family was just finishing supper when they heard the front door open and shut.

"There's Mom," said Robin.

Ann got up. "I'll get her helping out of the oven."

But before Ann could move, Alice was in the room. She stood in the doorway, looking very white and tired, but her eyes shone like stars.

"I've had a preview of your X ray, Lydie." She swallowed as though to fight back a sob. "It's good news. It looks as if you've made a perfect recovery."

Lydia looked and sounded amazed.

"Did anyone ever think that I wouldn't?" she said.

119

23   News from America

ALTHOUGH GEMMA'S MOTHER thought very little of amateur theatricals, she did her best to take an interest in anything that concerned her daughter. So in one of her letters she made a suggestion: "I can imagine what theatrical clothes made in the school will be like. I remember from that time I was in that film about Hampton Court how elaborate the clothes were of Lady Jane's date—all velvet and satin and embroidery. Will you tell that woman who has written the play that I'll foot the bill for your clothes? You can either rent them or get them made by a good theatrical dressmaker."

When Gemma had first come to live in Headstone, she would have jumped at her mother's suggestion, but without being conscious of it, she had learned a lot since. Even though she was the leading character in the play, that did not mean she must be the best dressed. After thinking it over, she showed the letter to Philip and Alice.

"I think the clothes they are making will be okay but, of course, not made of grand stuff like Mommy means."

"I read somewhere," Philip said, "that quite ordinary materials make up well for the stage."

"All the same," Alice said, "I think you should tell your Miss Jenkins about your mother's offer. It might be a great help having your clothes made outside, though goodness knows where we'd find a theatrical dressmaker."

120

"You can make it clear," Philip pointed out, "that you will be happy with the school designs but you thought she ought to know the offer had been made."

That evening after rehearsal Gemma spoke to Miss Jenkins. "I've had a letter from my mother; she's in America. She says she will pay for all my clothes to be made or rented. My uncle and aunt say I ought to tell you just in case you'd be glad."

Miss Jenkins had handed over the designing of the clothes to the school art department. The designs were then passed to Mrs. Paulson, the senior handicrafts teacher. Miss Jenkins knew from the groans which reached her that the handicrafts department was saying the art department expected miracles; how could the designs be carried out on the small amount of money they had to spend? As Gemma was talking, Miss Jekins had a vision of her dressed almost as Lady Jane would have been dressed, in the richest of materials covered in embroidery and precious stones. But in a flash she knew it couldn't be. What about Jane's parents and Queen Catherine Parr and the young Edward VI and the ladies and gentlemen of the court? How would they feel if Jane outdressed them all?

"It's very good of your mother to suggest it," Miss Jenkins said, feeling carefully for the right words, "but not practicable. You see, there's very little money to dress the whole cast, so I'm afraid there'll be a good deal of making do. It wouldn't do to have you dressed better than Queen Catherine or your own mother, would it?"

Gemma understood that, but what Miss Jekins had said gave her an idea. "Why don't I ask Mommy for the money and let it go toward all our clothes?"

Miss Jenkins could hardly believe her ears. "That would be wonderful, but would she? I mean, spending money on you is one thing, but on everybody is quite another. And I expect, like the rest of us, she has to count her pennies."

"Oh, no!" said Gemma. "She earns an awful lot." Too late she realized what she had said, so hurriedly she added: "You see, wages are high in America."

121

Unworldly Miss Jenkins was not interested in how Gemma's mother earned her living; she was interested only in the offer to help buy the clothes.

"Of course, I can't accept on my own account. This is a matter for Mr. Stevens, but if he should say yes, it would be a great help. It's the most generous idea, Gemma."

The next day Miss Jenkins saw Mr. Stevens and told him what Gemma had said. He started her by roaring with laughter.

"Gemma Robinson grows more mysterious every day. Now, not only is she able to give a wonderful imitation of a child who can speak both Greek and Latin, but she produces a mother who earns a lot of money in America. To add to it all, I gather she is quite willing to forgo being well dressed for the part herself in order to share the money with the whole cast. She's too good to be true."

"I must admit I was surprised that she didn't ask to be allowed to rent her dresses, but I think the reason is she is too good an artist not to see it would be impossible."

Mr. Stevens accepted that. "I think, Miss Jenkins, if Gemma can persuade her fabulous mother to cough up the money, we should accept. This play of yours is a very ambitious project, and we can do with all the help we can get. But if her mother sends money, it must be a secret where it comes from. Gemma must understand that."

So a letter went from Gemma to her mother. She had never taken so much trouble with a letter. She did not exactly admit that the money would help the whole cast, but she skirted around the point: "It would be glorious to wear really lovely clothes, but I couldn't be the only one. Some of the people I act with need to be dressed about as well as me or I would look wrong. But, Mommy, darling, if you could help about clothes, it would be gorgeous of you—one of the nicest things you ever did."

Lydia, much to her annoyance, could not go back to her dancing classes right away, but when she grasped what was expected of her in the exercise room at the hospital, she amazed everybody by the speed at which the injured hip got back its strength. As a result, it was not too long before Philip was telephoning Miss Arrowhead.

"They think at the hospital that Lydie can start her dancing classes again next week."

"Splendid!" Miss Arrowhead said. "But before she starts, I would like to have a word with you. Could you perhaps come in one evening when you are teaching down this way?"

Two days later Philip called on Miss Arrowhead. She was in her sitting room, and when she had given him a glass of sherry, she got straight down to the object of his visit. "Mrs. Robinson spoke to you about Lydie's education?"

Philip nodded. "Yes, I've not done anything about it because as you know, it was only too likely she would be unable to dance."

"But now that she was made this wonderful recovery, will you give your mind to a school for her in the autumn? I hear Mr. Stevens is considered a magnificent head of the Consolidated, but to me those huge day schools are like sausage machines: push the children in one end and hope they'll come out as alike as a pod of peas at the other. There is no room for—and no wish to cater to—the individual child."

"I'm afraid you are right." Philip agreed. "I shall have to move my niece, Gemma, in the autumn. She, too, needs a smaller school; she is not working as she should. A solution may be that we shall send both Gemma and Lydie to the same school if I can find one that is suitable."

"That is what I wanted to talk to you about." Miss Arrowhead smiled. "I'm sure you are going to shudder at this suggestion, but have you thought about the Drama School?"

Philip did shudder. "That place! What sort of education would the girls get there?"

"Good," aid Miss Arrowhead, "and I speak from experience. I have a young niece, Polly, working with me. Her parents are dead—a flying accident. Her father was an actor, so when I took the child to live with me, thinking she might want to follow in his footsteps, I sent her there. As it happened, she was more interested in dancing."

Philip could not believe a drama school could be good educationally. "I will look at the school for Gemma, but it will be no good for Lydie. I couldn't just send one child to a paying school."

"That is what I wanted to talk to you about. Without giving her name, I had a word with Mrs. Calvert, who runs the school, about Lydie. I think she would give her a free place."

Philip looked at Miss Arrowhead with a twinkle in his eyes. "When you want something, you go all out for it, don't you?"

"Yes, when I see real talent. Without straining, if she goes to the Drama School, Lydie can have her timetable so arranged that she can do a full week's work as well as train to be a dancer."

Philip got up. "I promise you I will go and look and make inquiries about the Drama School. I can't say more at present."

Philip came home deep in thought. Of course, Robin was at a paying school, but he had won a scholarship. In a way, if on Miss Arrowhead's advice Mrs. Calvert gave Lydia a place in the Drama School, that would be a kind of scholarship, but what about Ann? It needed a lot of thinking out.

As Philip reached home, Gemma rushed down the stairs, waving a slip of paper. "You'll never guess what this is. Mommy has sent a hundred pounds for clothes for Lady Jane. Isn't it too marvelous to be true! I should think Miss Jenkins will drop dead when she knows. And Mommy says that if I am happy at Headstone Consolidated, I needn't move; she says it's my being happy she cares about."

Philip could well believe that was exactly what Rowena had written and was how she felt, but he was not going to have Gemma growing up an ignoramus if he could help it. However, this was not the moment to argue with her, so all he said was: "A hundred pounds! What a generous present! I'm so glad, Gemma."

24 ❧ On the Block

HOW HE MANAGED it Miss Jenkins never knew, but Mr. Stevens passed the hundred pounds to the drama group without divulging where it came from. The excitement was intense, and of course, there was gossip, but that Gemma had anything to do with it was kept a dead secret. Still, the effects of the money were felt immediately, by both those who were working on the clothes and those who were working on the scenery and the stage properties, for they suddenly discovered they could have more or less what was needed.

The result was as if everybody had been injected with a syringeful of energy. There had been class projects appliquéing yards of scenery onto canvas, which had been discussed but had not got off the ground. Furniture was to be painted and upholstered. Coats of arms were to be designed and decorated. Now everything got started. As for the clothes department, it was such a different proposition to discover that within reason you could have what you asked for that even halfhearted seamstresses got interested and offered extra time, and those who were really clever with their fingers asked permission to take headdresses and girdles home to embroider or decorate with beads.

Quite soon Gemma was told to come for fittings. These were held in the art room. Many girls who found themselves standing in their underwear while quite senior girls knelt around them pinning and snipping would have been embarrassed. But to Gemma, used to fittings since she was a baby, there was nothing to it. She stood perfectly still, neither complaining nor fidgeting, exactly as she had done when taken to her film company's wardrobe for fittings. As a rule she spent fitting time going over her lines in her head, especially the difficult scenes where she spoke Latin and Greek with her tutor. Her patience amazed both Mrs. Paulson, the head of handicrafts, and the girls who fitted her.

"Are you tired, Gemma?" they would say, or "Shout if a pin gets into you."

Gemma had to pull herself away from her part to answer: "I'm fine, thank you."

"What a curious child," said Mrs. Paulson. "If I hadn't seen her in the pageant, I should say she couldn't say a line on a stage. She seems so dreamy and silent."

Sometimes Gemma surprised them. She was interested in nothing but the smooth running of the play. This, of course, included her looking well and suitably dressed on all occasions. But in some scenes other things mattered. One day, when she was being fitted for a blue velvet dress with the front stiff with beads, she asked: "Do you know which scene this is for?"

One of the girls consulted a list. "Act Two, Scene Three."

"Then wait a second," said Gemma. "This design may have to be altered. That is a scene between me and my cousin Edward the Sixth. Even though we're cousins, I have to be fearfully formal—like this."

Gemma moved away and pretended to come in at a door. As she entered, she curtsied three times as if her cousin were present and then knelt, as she had to do, to speak to him.

"There's an awful lot of kneeling in this scene for beads. I should think I'd break them at the first dress rehearsal."

Mrs. Paulson and the girl seamstresses went into a huddle, and in the end it was decided to embroider the front of the dress. But when Gemma had gone, Mrs. Paulson said: "What a strange child. Standing like a dummy so you wouldn't think she cared what she wore. Then suddenly she comes out with information as she did today."

A school play was considered an outside school activity and was not supposed to interfere with schoolwork. But the class 3 form teacher, Miss Smith, though she was sympathetic and had helped by reducing Gemma's homework, never stopped complaining. "Unless your work improves, Gemma, I shall have to ask the drama group not to use you in future productions."

But what Miss Smith said was wasted on Gemma. She was by now so involved in Lady Jane very little else filtered through to her.

As the term progressed, rehearsals lengthened. There were performances on a Thursday, a Friday, and twice on Saturday at the end of May. This meant that the play must be almost ready for production before the Easter holidays. Then, at the beginning of the next term, they could polish up any scene that needed it, ready for the dress rehearsals, for which there would be two.

By now all the scenes had been seen by the drama group except the final one. This only concerned Jane; Nurse Ellen, who had looked after her since babyhood; a Mrs. Tilney, who also waited on her; the lieutenant of the Tower; and the headsman. There had historically been many more people present, but Miss Jenkins had decided to keep the scene as short and simple as possible. At one rehearsal when most of the cast was present, they asked to stay to see the last scene. Miss Jenkins could not refuse, but she was shy about this scene. She had written it with sincerity, sticking strictly to part of what Jane had actually said, and insofar as was possible, she had not written with emotion. She looked at Mr. Weldon to see how he felt as producer; he gave her an encouraging nod.

"Yes, stay by all means. It's time you saw how the play ends. Places, everybody."

They were already using the headsman's block they would use in the play. The previous scene had finished with Jane in her prison cell. She had just watched the cart with her husband Guilford's bloodstained body and severed head go by the window. In the last scene she was discovered standing in front of the block, from where she addressed the audience as if they were the crowd on Tower Hill. "Good people," she had to say, "I am come here to die. My

127

offense against the queen's Highness, which is now deemed treason, was never of my seeking but by counsel of those who would have further understanding of these things than I, which knew little of the law, and much less to the titles to the crown. But touching the procurement and desire thereof by me, or on my behalf, I do wash my hands in innocency here of before God, and in the fact of all you good Christian people. And now, good people, while I am alive, I pray you assist me with your prayers."

By this time Nurse Ellen and Mrs. Tilney were crying so dreadfully neither was capable of tying the scarf around Jane's eyes. The headsman knelt and had to say, "Do you forgive me, Madam?" to which Jane replied, "Most willingly."

Then Jane herself tied the scarf around her eyes and fumbled, feeling for the way to the block. There she had to kneel, but even as the executioner lifted his ax, she raised her head to say: "Lord, into thy hands I commend my spirit."

"Curtain," said Mr. Weldon.

Gemma ran home so happy she felt drunk. Nobody had said a word at the end of the rehearsal, but there had been a lot of mopped eyes, and even some of the boys were sniffing. This was what she had dreamed would happen.

I made them cry, Gemma sang in her head. *I made them cry*.

In Trelawny Drive she had to come down to earth a little; she couldn't hope the cousins would understand what a glorious thing had happened. Still, they would know the next term when they saw the play.

The family were in the sitting room, all talking at once. Lydia looked up as Gemma came in.

"Oh, Gemma, something smashing has happened!"

Robin was jumping around the room he was so excited. "Mr. Rumage has said we can have the Winter Garden."

"What for?" Gemma asked.

Ann looked shocked. "Don't say you've forgotten! It's for the concert for the dog for the blind. We're doing it this holidays."

128

25 ❧ A Dog for the Blind

THERE WERE, Gemma discovered, a lot of reasons why the concert for the dog for the blind should take place in the Easter holidays. First, the school choir, which was taking no part in *Lady Jane*, had quite a long program ready and would like to share the concert with Gemma and Sisters. Secondly, the conductor of the school choir was a friend of Mr. Rumage's, and he had been given the offer of the loan of the Winter Garden for a performance after Easter. Finally, Miss Arrowhead had said she did not think Lydia's tutu was suitable for the sleep fairy, which Lydia was dancing in her ballet, but she would teach her a dance for which she could wear it as an extra turn at the concert for the dog for the blind.

"And you do see, Gemma," Lydia explained, "I simply must wear it now because otherwise I won't get a chance until perhaps next Christmas, because Miss Arrowhead's ballet is in the summer, and by Christmas I might have outgrown it."

Gemma could see all the reasons for the concert and that they were good, but a concert just now was the last thing she wanted. There would be new songs to learn apart from "I Saw Three Ships," which she was already working on. There would be a lot of rehearsals needed, for really it would mean giving two complete performances—one in each half. Luckily for Gemma the performance was fixed for the last week of the holiday, so she was able to say firmly that there could be no rehearsals until the holiday started.

"Then we can have one almost every day if you like."

In this Gemma was backed up by Ann. "I couldn't rehearse until the holidays either; you see, there's extra school choir rehearsals, for I'm singing with them, of course."

As it happened, the hard work for Gemma and Sisters was just—though she didn't know it—what Gemma needed. It was a case of the round and round curing the up and down. She was so busy with rehearsals that all through the Easter holidays she had very little time to spare for Lady Jane, and this meant the part did not get stale, which it well might have done had she worked at it all through the holidays.

It was fortunate for them all that Philip had promised performances of Gemma and Sisters for several organizations before the big concert had been arranged. This meant that all the new material could be tried out. This was a great help to Gemma, who, terribly conscious of the smallness of her singing voice and how little she knew about banjo playing, shook like a jelly the first time she sang "I Saw Three Ships" in public. But she soon learned she need not worry; it went over just as well as "There Was a Lady Loved a Swine."

"There, you see," said Ted, "what did I tell you? Before next winter when you've finished with this Lady Jane Grey lark, I'll have you with a rep of six songs, see if I don't."

But singing to the banjo was not Gemma's only trouble about the big concert. It was the layout of the whole program. Of course, there had to be other performers besides the school choir and Gemma and Sisters, and she found when she first saw the suggested program that no one had remembered that both Ann and Lydia had to have time to change. The school choir wore the school uniform of gray pleated skirts, white blouses, and purple ties. Gemma and Sisters had been planned to finish the first half, meaning they followed a group of songs by the choir. In the second half Lydia's solo dance was placed just before Gemma and Sisters.

The proposed program was sent to Philip from Mr. Rumage. It

arrived during breakfast, so he passed it to Gemma, who at once started to storm. "Have they gone mad? It needs at least five minutes for Ann to get out of her school uniform and into her black plastic, and Lydia needs every bit of that to get out of her tutu. Why can't they think?"

"Keep your hair on," said Philip. "This program is clearly marked 'suggested' and 'for approval.' I'll ring Mr. Rumage after breakfast and ask if we may see him to sort things out."

Mr. Rumage was a calm man.

"Okay," he said when he heard Gemma's troubles. "So we've got to shift somebody so they come on between the choir and all the singing you do in Gemma and Sisters. I've got it! There's that accordion player, we'll put him in there." He blue-penciled the program. "Now, Lydie, that's easy: She can dance before the choir sings, not after. Any other troubles?"

Gemma felt she had made fuss about nothing. "No. You've made it seem easy, but I felt despairing when I first saw the program."

Mr. Rumage gave Gemma a friendly grin. "When you've been in the business as long as I have, you'll find worrying does no good. When I was first in show biz, I was manager of a film theater. Well, one Christmas we were promised a big attraction—the star of the film would appear in person; it was Rowena Alston."

Gemma gave a quick look at Philip. There was the smallest sign of a smile at the corners of his mouth, but that was all.

"Didn't she turn up?" he asked.

"Not her fault. The film company muddled the date; she was sent to the wrong theater."

Gemma remembered the incident, her mother coming home in the most towering temper, so angry it had woken Gemma up. She had crept into the sitting room in her dressing gown to find her mother in full evening dress and a mink cape, storming up and down.

"Imagine what a fool I looked," she was telling Miss Court, "dressed like this! And the manager didn't even know who I was. Can you believe that? I'll ring my agents in the morning and tell them what they can do to the company. I'll tear up my contract. They can't treat me like this."

Gemma had not before thought about what the manager of the cinema at which her mother should have appeared had thought.

"What did you do?" she asked.

Mr. Rumage made a dismissing gesture. "What could I do? The house was packed. I came on the stage and apologized. I didn't then know what had happened, so I said Rowena Alston was ill and offered them their money back. If anyone at that moment had had a tomato on them, it would have been thrown at me."

In the car driving home Philip said to Gemma: "I thought we carried that off very well. But, as my mother would say, 'Oh, what a fearful web we weave when once we practice to deceive.' I shall be glad when you decide to use your own name."

Gemma did not answer that, but she thought: *And that will be never. As long as I live in Headstone, I'm not going to let anybody know I was once a film star.*

The performance to buy a dog for the blind was a great success. Although the affair had been got up in a hurry, all the tickets were sold, for the pupils of Headstone Consolidated undertook the selling. The audience loved both performances of Gemma and Sisters, and it certainly went very well. Gemma sang her new song in the first half.

"I just couldn't have it hanging over me all the evening," she explained to Ann.

Gemma need not have worried; the audience loved "I Saw Three Ships," as they loved everything the girls did, but the great success of the show was Robin's swirled songs helped out by Nigs on the drums. These, since more than half the audience were teenagers, were greeted with shouts and whistles, and all four songs had to be sung twice.

But the high spot of the evening came right at the end. A blind man was led onto the stage by his guide dog, a splendid, capable-looking Labrador with which everybody fell in love. Then the man made a little speech. He told the audience that his dog, Edward, was the best friend anyone ever had, that he could not imagine life without him. "But tonight," he said, "everybody here has helped to give somebody an Edward. A dog for a blind person costs two hundred and fifty pounds, and that is what has been made this evening."

As usual there was a grand going-over of the performance at supper while the children simmered down.

"I'm awfully glad we got enough for a whole dog," said Ann. "Eunice ought to give us a lot of house marks with you in the show, Gemma."

Lydia had been carried away by the glory of seeing herself in a tutu. "There's got to be another concert, there absolutely must, at which I can wear my tutu before I outgrow it," she insisted. "Everybody said it looked marvelous."

Alice had been so thrilled that Lydia could dance at all that she had scarcely noticed the dress, but she said: "Don't worry, darling, you don't grow much, and anyway, it will let out."

Gemma did not join in the discussion. She was tired out; though it had been fun, she was glad the concert was over. Now she could once more give all of herself to Lady Jane.

26 ❦ The Drama School

OUTWARDLY THE summer term at Headstone Consolidated began like any other summer term. The games changed: Away went the footballs and hockey sticks, and out came the cricket bats and pads and the tennis rackets. The uniform changed, too; in spite of the fact that the weather was cold, the girls wore their cotton dresses under their school blazers, and no boy was seen in the uniform pullover. Yet underneath it was not an ordinary summer term, and it would not be until the end of May after the production of *Lady Jane Grey*.

Most years at some time the drama group produced a play, but *Lady Jane Grey* was different. First of all, it was a new play written by a teacher in the school; this alone assured it of interest well beyond the school walls. Then it was a far more ambitious effort than anything before attempted; this meant that in one way or another a very large proportion of the school was involved.

Nor was it only the teachers and pupils of the school who were knee-deep in the production; so were the families of the actors, and none more than the Robinsons.

"Oh, goodness!" said Lydia to Alice. "You can't think how I wish that awful Lady Jane was over, because I know none of you will be properly interested in my dance in Miss Arrowhead's ballet until it is."

134

"How can you say that?" Alice protested. "What's that in tissue paper on the sewing machine?"

Lydia was to wear a gray silk tunic as the sleep fairy, and Alice was making it.

"Oh, I know you're making my frock," Lydia said, "but I mean being interested, asking questions and things."

Robin heard this conversation. "I know exactly what Lydie means. That miserable Lady Jane, who I hate more every day, is like Christmas—we're measuring things by her. You know—before Lady Jane or after Lady Jane."

"Never mind, darlings." Alice comforted them. "It's not long now, and I promise you, Lydie, we shall all be just as excited when your ballet is coming along."

All the same Alice knew there was truth in the children's complaints. As an example almost every day Philip would say: "We must make an appointment to go and see Mrs. Calvert at the Drama School." But he had not made one because no decision about a change of school could be made without Gemma, for her mother was certain to write to her about it, and Gemma was in no state to think about changing schools.

However, in the end Alice did make Philip telephone and an appointment was made, and on the following Saturday they drove off to meet Mrs. Calvert.

The Drama School had a building in no way comparable to Headstone Consolidated. It was two Victorian houses thrown into one. This gave one long main hall with a stage and many small classrooms. Compared to the consolidated school, it was gloomy and dark. But it had an atmosphere which at once came over to Philip and Alice.

Mrs. Calvert, so her secretary told them, would be with them in a few minutes, and they were shown into her sitting room to wait. It was a pretty room furnished with good furniture and yellow curtains and chair covers. Alice prowled around, trying to visualize Lydia in the school.

"It smells nice, I think," she said to Philip. "You know, none of that rather antiseptic smell big schools have."

135

Somewhere somebody was either practicing or having a violin lesson. Philip had unconsciously paused in the hall to listen. "Whoever is playing the fiddle was properly taught."

"When we talk to Mrs. Calvert about Gemma," Alice asked, "are we calling her Robinson? I know she goes to her tap classes as Gemma Robinson, but I doubt if Mrs. Calvert would know it was the same child."

Philip frowned. "I hope just to call her my niece, Gemma. There's no point in upsetting her before her play comes on by telling her we are planning to change her school, still less that I want her to use her own name. I have hinted, as you know, that both things might happen, but while she's so involved with the play, I doubt if she's taken my hints in."

Before Alice could answer, the door opened and Mrs. Calvert came in.

Mrs. Calvert was an arresting-looking woman. She had red hair looped over her cheeks as worn in Queen Victoria's day and fastened in a soft bun at the back of her neck. She was wearing a dress that for some reason looked vaguely period; it was modern yet gave a feeling it would not look out of place in a Shakespearean play.

After shaking hands with Philip and Alice, she sat down at her desk. She had a deep voice and enunciated her words clearly. "Miss Arrowhead is a very old friend, and she has talked to me about your daughter. She sounds like a very talented child. We do teach dancing, but if you entrust Lydia to me, I shall so arrange her curriculum that she spends the first hour every morning with Miss Arrowhead and later, of course, longer."

Philip said: "We have heard of your very generous offer to help Lydie, but really what has brought us here today is my niece. We are not satisfied that Gemma is the right child for a big consolidated school."

"There is plenty of money," Alice hastened to explain. "It's a smaller school we think she needs."

"More individual attention," Philip added.

"But this is a drama school," Mrs. Calvert pointed out. "Has this niece any interest in the theater?"

To Alice and Philip this was downright funny.

"Oh, yes," Alice said. "She was the girl in the pageant. I expect you saw it."

Mrs. Calvert nodded. "Oh, was she! Yes, I remember thinking she was a gifted child."

Philip said: "And she's playing the part of Lady Jane Grey in the play of that name that Headstone Consolidated is putting on this month."

"Indeed!" Mrs. Calvert nodded. "I am going to see that. Most interesting that it should be written by a local woman."

It was so clear that to Mrs. Calvert what was interesting was the fact that a teacher had written the play rather than who was acting what part that Philip and Alice were momentarily silenced. It seemed so odd to hear the part of Lady Jane dismissed like that after living with her for so long. After a pause Philip said: "Although Gemma is good at acting, it's her schoolwork that I am particularly anxious about."

At once Mrs. Calvert got down to business. She produced time-tables and lists of teachers, almost all of whom had good degrees.

"Don't think for a second, Mr. Robinson, that because we teach acting and the allied arts that general education suffers. Quite the contrary. We are very A-level-conscious."

Philip smiled. "I'm not sure that isn't reaching a bit high for my niece, Gemma."

"We shall see," said Mrs. Calvert, speaking, Alice noticed, as if Gemma were already her pupil. "And now, if you will come with me, I will show you over the school, starting with the bottom classes, in one of which no doubt Lydia will work. I take no pupils before they are nine."

Driving home, Alice—after discussing the school very favorably, for both she and Philip had liked it—said: "I have a feeling that Lydie and Gemma will be going there in the autumn. I think Mrs. Calvert is arranging it."

Philip laughed. "There are other schools we could see."

"I daresay," said Alice. "But you mark my words, it is to Mrs. Calvert they will go and nowhere else."

27 ❦ Lady Jane Grey

ALL THOSE IN Headstone interested in the theater were excited about the production of *Lady Jane Grey*. Miss Jenkins, pink with embarrassment, was interviewed and photographed, to be described in the local paper as "Headstone's Playwright."

Although the tickets were charged for, the money to go toward building the school a real theater, Mr. Stevens insisted on having the two front rows at the first performance for school guests. These included the conductor of the Steen and his wife, Miss Arrowhead, Mrs. Calvert and her husband, who was said to be a business tycoon, the chief librarian, and other town dignitaries supposed to be interested in the arts. Mr. Stevens, wishing to enjoy himself, put Miss Arrowhead to sit on his right side, for he took pleasure in her caustic humor.

"I feel quite nervous," he confessed to Miss Arrowhead. "So much work has gone into this play, and I would so dislike it if Miss Jenkins was disappointed. There is a rumor there is the theater critic of one of the national papers in the audience. I'm afraid poor Miss Jenkins's first attempt at a play will scarcely stand up to that."

Presently the lights went down, and the curtain rose to a storm of applause. The handicrafts department had excelled itself. The scene was laid in part of the great hall at Bradgate, Lady Jane's home. To give the effect of riches, a huge tapestry had been designed and appliquéd onto canvas. In front of it stood what appeared to be an elaborately carved table and some chairs, which had been made by the boys in the carpenter's shop. The scene was between Jane's difficult, arrogant mother and her good-looking but much weaker father. They were discussing Jane's education. It came out in the conversation that Jane at the time was nearly nine. Presently Jane was summoned to be told that she was to leave home for two years. She was to be sent to Queen Catherine Parr.

To get over the age difficulty, Gemma started the play with flat shoes and gradually wore higher heels to show she was growing up. Since children of the aristocracy of that date wore replicas of adult clothes, there was no other way of aging Gemma except through her acting. To help, a very tall boy and girl had been chosen to play the Dorset parents, and this was a success because in spite of her elaborate scarlet gown with its bell-shaped skirt and slashed sleeves, Gemma managed to look like a little girl. Having made her curtsies, she waited to hear what was to be said to her.

One of Gemma's great assets, which had endeared her to her screen public, was her aloof, wistful quality. This was very telling in the first scene, for she had little to say; at that date you did not argue with your parents. But as Gemma heard of the two years to be spent at court, her misery at the prospect of leaving her home could be read on her face, so already with very little said she had the audience in her hands.

Scene followed scene with remarkable rapidity for a school play. The tapestries of the great hall at Bradgate came down and were replaced by scenes in first Whitehall, and later, after Henry VIII's death, Queen Catherine Parr's house at Wimbledon. The act finished with the death of the young King Edward VI.

There was tremendous applause as the curtain fell, and after it roars of conversation. There was no doubt about it: Miss Jenkins had written a gripping play, and Gemma was giving a startlingly good performance.

Mr. Stevens invited his front rows of guests to come outside and have a cup of coffee, but before they moved, Miss Arrowhead touched his arm. "Young Gemma is certainly remarkable, but shouldn't we expect her to be?"

Mr. Stevens looked surprised. "Should we?"

"Don't tell me you haven't spotted who she is."

Mr. Stevens shook his head. "No."

"That is Gemma Bow."

Mr. Stevens slapped his hands together. "Of course. I knew I had heard that voice before and seen that face. I coached the child in these scenes you have just watched where she talked Latin and Greek—I hope you noticed the ease with which she spoke but, alas, it's all learned like a parrot—well, at the end of each coaching I racked my brains trying to recall where I had seen and heard her before."

They were moving toward the coffee.

"Don't you remember her at about the age of eight wringing the nation's heart as a child in an orphanage?"

"Yes, indeed. That's the film that's been haunting me."

Miss Arrowhead paused. "I think we keep our knowledge to ourselves for the moment, don't you?"

"Right," said Mr. Stevens. "Come on, everybody, or you won't get your coffee before the curtain goes up."

The next act opened with the scene where Gemma as Jane first heard of the young king's death and that she was to be proclaimed queen. The double news so appalled her that she almost fainted and finally burst into tears. When she had recovered, she had to say to the duke of Northumberland: "The lady Mary is the rightful heir." Finally, after pressure from her parents, she gave in and, kneeling, asked God for guidance. It was a long and difficult scene and, as Miss Jenkins had pointed out at rehearsals, very important historically, so Gemma was scared of it and needed to prepare herself for it. Several of the girls from the needlework classes were acting as dressers, but Miss Jenkins herself dressed Gemma. She had watched her at rehearsals and knew how important it was to her to hold the mood from one scene to another. Chatter might easily upset her. When Gemma was dressed, she helped her to

140

sit in a chair without crushing her dress and brought her a cup of tea.

"Drink that, dear, and rest here until the act starts; nobody will disturb you." Then, carried away, she gave Gemma a kiss. "You are splendid, dear! Splendid!"

Act Two held the audience gripped. Gemma, by now in high heels, was every inch a queen. The scenes in the White Tower, during which she was supposed to rule, were touching in the extreme, for in spite of the girl's dignity, she was so pitifully young. The act finished with the end of the nine days of Jane's reign and the news that she and her husband, Guilford Dudley, were to be tried for high treason.

There was less noise in the second intermission. Many of the audience had been in tears, and the knowledge that they now had to watch the tragic end didn't cheer them up.

"I do hope we don't see her with her head on the block," one woman whispered to another. Philip, Alice, Ann, Lydia, and Robin were smothering under the praise heaped on Gemma. Not going in for extravagant talk themselves, they found it embarrassing.

"Yes, she is good, isn't she?" Alice murmured.

"Yes, she's splendid," Philip said over and over again. Then, trying to be honest: "Her mother's good; it's in the blood."

Robin, who had been bored to death, waited for a pause in the congratulations; then he leaned across Lydia to hiss fiercely: "How they do go on. Me, I've been bored! Bored! Bored! I knew I would be; only it's worse than I expected. Must I stay to the end? Couldn't I go home?"

"Me too," said Lydia. "Honestly, Dad, I don't ever want to see Lady Jane again."

Philip laughed. "You're a couple of Philistines, and you certainly can't go home before the end. What do you think of the play, Ann?"

Ann had been so carried away that while the curtain was up, she had forgotten it was Gemma she was watching and thought of her only as Lady Jane. "I love it, and I think Gemma is perfect—she's so good I can't find the words to explain."

"You don't have to," Alice whispered. "Here come Mrs. Glesse and Rosie."

Mrs. Glesse was very gracious. "My dear Mr. and Mrs. Robinson, I said to Rosie we really must congratulate them, for Gemma is excellent, quite excellent. Of course, a sad story like this tells itself, not much acting called for, but I must say she takes her part ever so nicely."

Meanwhile, solace had come to Robin and Lydia. They saw Nigs's red head coming toward them.

"Dad and Mom made me come," he said. "They said it was educational, but it's even worse than you said it would be, Robin. But I came prepared." Then out of his pocket he produced a wonderful assortment of whipped cream walnuts, Mars bars, and packages of sweets. "If you eat carefully, nobody will notice you're doing it. Just lean forward with your mouth behind your hand."

Lydia had to be fair. "Have you got some left for yourself?"

"I don't want any more," said Nigs proudly. "Anyway, I bought them for you. And as a matter of fact, I have still got half a Mars bar. If I eat it slowly, it will last until the end. It can't be long now. Anyway, I shall like seeing her head cut off."

The last act began. The scene was Jane's prison in the Tower. Miss Jenkins had allowed her imagination full play in this act. She was sure in those last hours Jane would have thought back to her lovely home, Bradgate, and she and her old nurse would talk about it. In the play Miss Jenkins made poor old Nurse Ellen, between her sobs, sew clean ruffles into the neck and sleeves of the black dress Jane was to wear to the block.

The audience was terribly moved, and when the last scene started, many women had their handkerchiefs in readiness. Gemma delivered her speech to the crowd on Tower Hill quite beautifully, and when, as she raised her head from the block to say, "Lord, into thy hands I commend my spirit," there was, discounting Robin, Nigs, and Lydia, hardly a dry eye in the hall. It was almost a relief when the curtain fell.

Never had the hall heard such applause. The audience stamped

142

and clapped and shouted "bravo." At a drama group performance none of the actors took separate calls. They stood in rows, bowing. Gemma would hardly have noticed if the audience had hissed, for she was so strung up, but she did register the shout of applause for Miss Jenkins and the cries of "speech."

Oh, I'm so glad it's a success for her, Gemma thought. *So terribly glad.*

28 ❦ Gemma Bow

GEMMA HAD GIVEN so much to Lady Jane that the Sunday after the last performance she collapsed. She got out of bed to come down to breakfast and fainted. Ann, coming back from the bathroom, found her lying on the floor.

Alice, answering Ann's scream for help, found Gemma just opening her eyes.

"It's all right, chickabiddy," she said. "You are overtired. Let us get you back into bed."

Gemma, on the advice of the doctor, spent three days in bed.

"She's just exhausted," he told Alice. "Nothing rest won't cure." He had seen *Lady Jane Grey*, so he added: "That was a very big part for a small girl, and it's taken a lot out of her."

Gemma was furious at being kept away from school. She had expected a heroine's entrance on the Monday. It would be the school's chance to tell her now how good she had been. Only too well she knew that by the time she got back on Wednesday the first excitement would have died down, and likely enough everybody's interest would be focused on something else.

Philip took advantage of Gemma's being in bed to talk to her about the Drama School. He came into the bedroom on the Tuesday afternoon between classes and sat on Ann's bed.

144

"Your aunt and I went to have a look at the Drama School a week or two ago."

Gemma was surprised.

"What for?"

"We were giving it a look-over, not only as a possible school for you but for Lydie."

Gemma was offended. "Why should I want to go to a place like that?" She didn't say, "What acting could they teach me?" but she meant it.

"I think you might be happy there. I haven't thought about it from the acting viewpoint but from the educational point of view. They have a very high standard there. The examination results are most creditable."

Gemma had seen the school only as an outsider attending tap classes. She had never thought about it as a proper school. In any case she did not want to move from the consolidated school. She was somebody there now.

"Who says I've got to move? Mommy hasn't written any more about it."

Philip spoke kindly, but his voice was firm. "You aren't getting on at the consolidated, are you?"

Gemma thought that mean. "Well, you couldn't expect anything startling while I was working on Lady Jane, could you?"

"You have worked on Lady Jane in only the last few months, but you haven't got out of that bottom stream since you went to the school."

"I've moved up twice."

"It's more or less automatic that you move up in each autumn term."

"Nobody at school seems worried," Gemma said sulkily.

"They may not have said so, but I don't think they look upon you as a show pupil, do they?"

Gemma thought about that. Miss Smith had been very kind lately, knowing about Lady Jane, but she had said at intervals: "You'll have to work very hard, Gemma, after the play to make up all the work you have missed." She had not said, "Or you won't get

145

moved this autumn," but it was hinted. Not to be moved with the rest of the class was the ultimate shame and usually happened only to those who were unteachable. At the time Gemma had brushed what Miss Smith had said aside; after the play felt like years away, a date that would never come. Now, with her uncle's eyes boring into her, Miss Smith's words came back, and they weren't nice to remember.

"Now the play's over, I can work all out."

"Will you?"

Would she? Too well Gemma knew herself. She would mean to work hard, but she seemed temperamentally incapable of working at subjects she didn't like.

"I'll do my best, honestly I will."

"I don't believe that's good enough," Philip said. "I'm not altogether blaming you; lots of boys and girls need individual attention, which is impossible to arrange in a big school. You are in your best subjects working below your capacity because your classwork is geared to the ability of the lowest. Now, if in the autumn you go to the Drama School and you are found to be below standard in any subject, you get private coaching."

"But I don't want to go to the Drama School. I've made myself a person at Headstone Consolidated."

Philip smiled. "I've thought of that. I don't suppose you should go there under my name. You must use your own."

Gemma had been Robinson so long that the idea of becoming Gemma Bow once more took her breath away. Still, it was a thought. Gemma Bow! There would be no need to worry about being somebody in the Drama School when they knew who she was. It was unlikely they'd ever had a film star there before. Gemma grinned at her uncle.

"I could explain I'd given up working in pictures because of my education."

"That's the idea." Philip agreed. "You can, if you like, tell them about Headstone Consolidated when you get to know them. All film stars are allowed to do unusual things; you'll get away with it."

"Why's Lydie coming too?"

"It's her dancing. Miss Arrowhead arranged it. Mrs. Calvert is taking her for nothing. She is to go to Miss Arrowhead for the first hour every morning."

"Well, that seems a good idea." Gemma smiled conspiratorially at Philip. "If you don't mind my saying so, you are a bit of a schemer, aren't you? Still, I like the scheme, and I think it will work out."

As Gemma had feared, the first excitement about her Lady Jane had worn off when she returned to school, but she got sufficient praise to keep her happy. There was also good news to give Ann. Eunice had come to her in the lunch break and had said in her gruff voice: "We all thought you did a smashing job as Lady Jane. We had a special meeting, and you've been awarded ten house marks. That means Dickens's House is almost certain to win the cup. Pretty good my last term as House Captain."

A few days later Mr. Stevens sent for Gemma. To her, after being coached by him, he was now more a friend than a headmaster, so she went to his room without a qualm. She was quite right, for he smiled at her as she came in.

"Sit down, Gemma. I have heard from your uncle that you are leaving us next term."

"That's right," Gemma said. "I'm being sent to that drama school. Uncle Philip thinks I need special coaching, especially in math. I'm a dumb clot at it."

"We shall be sorry to lose you—you were admirable as Lady Jane. All the same, I think a drama school is the right place for Gemma Bow."

Gemma gaped at him. "How long have you known?"

"At the back of my head ever since you first came to the school, for I had seen some of your films and I knew I had seen you before, but it was Miss Arrowhead from the dancing school who actually spotted who you were."

"You haven't told anybody, have you? I'll be Gemma Bow at the new school, but I don't want to be here."

"That's all right, your secret is safe with me. Well, that's all. I really only wanted to congratulate you."

Gemma felt it was only polite to tell Miss Jenkins she was leaving. She expected her to be upset at the thought of the drama group without her, but Miss Jenkins took the news calmly, for she was starry-eyed with her own affairs. Somebody from the BBC television had seen *Lady Jane Grey* and wanted to adapt it as a TV play.

"We shall miss you, dear," she said, "but I'm sure you'll enjoy the Drama School. Far more opportunities for acting."

Lydia was enchanted to hear she was going to the Drama School. "Imagine a lesson every morning with Miss Arrowhead! It's too perfect to be true. It seems mean you can't go there, too, Ann."

Ann looked appalled. "Thank you very much but I'd hate it. I'd loathe to learn to act, and I love Headstone Consolidated. I never want to leave."

Philip, who heard this, said: "You may have another thought if you get a scholarship to the Royal College of Music."

"I doubt it," Ann retorted. "I like things as they are. I don't want to go away to London."

"I'm glad I've got the new school to look forward to," Gemma said, "or I'd feel flat, as if nothing nice would ever happen again now Lady Jane's over."

Lydia turned a neat pirouette. "Nothing nice! I like that! Has Miss Gemma Bow not noticed that in three weeks is Miss Arrowhead's ballet starring Little Miss Lydia Robinson?"

29 ଓ And What Next?

MISS ARROWHEAD'S ballet was a great success. It would not be true to say that to most of the audience Lydia was the star, for the Winter Garden was crammed with moms, dads, grandmothers, grandfathers, uncles, aunts, and cousins, each of whom knew his or her particular rabbit, gnome, fairy, or flower had danced everybody else off the stage.

Of course, Gran was staying with the Robinsons for the occasion. The ballet was performed on Saturday afternoon, so she arrived on the Saturday morning and before lunch had already produced five proverbs. To Gemma and Lydia, when she heard about the new school, "Birds of a feather flock together." To Alice, when she offered to help get the lunch, "Many hands make light work." To Lydia, when she showed her the tutu, "Fine feathers make fine birds." To Robin, when he told her how tough Nigs's parents were about allowing him to practice his drums, "It's the last straw that breaks the camel's back." To Ann, when she told her that her father hoped later on she would win a musical scholarship, not to worry, as "There's many a slip 'twixt cup and lip."

When Alice took a protesting Robin into the bathroom to clean him up for the matinee, he said: "I'd say Gran was more than up to form, wouldn't you, Mom?"

Alice laughed. "She's certainly strong on proverbs today."

149

"If I knew one about having to watch things you don't want to watch, I'd say it now," said Robin. "I shouldn't wonder if this matinee was worse than that awful *Lady Jane Grey*."

Alice handed him the towel. "For goodness' sake, don't mention that play to Gran; she'll hate to hear about it and will take it out on poor Gemma."

In spite of Miss Arrowhead's calling her effort, "a horrid little ballet," in its simple way it was rather charming, and the final scene where all the characters were sent to sleep by Lydia really delightful. Mr. Rumage's stage lightning was used to the full, fading from a pink sunset to dusk to the light of a slowly rising moon. While the lights changed, like a will-o'-the-wisp Lydia danced, a flitting, twirling gray shadow. The actual arrangement of steps was not difficult, but Lydia produced a kind of magic, for the qualities that make an outstanding dancer as a rule show early. As she watched Lydia, unashamed Alice had tears pouring down her cheeks. It could so easily have been another child dancing while Lydia, crippled, could only sit and watch.

Alice was not the only one to cry. Miss Arrowhead, who prided herself on her toughness, was caught in the wings by Polly, mopping her eyes.

"Isn't she perfect?" Polly whispered. "Of course, she's got a lot to learn, but if she goes on improving, she might finish anywhere, mightn't she?"

"How true," Miss Arrowhead said. "And to think how nearly she had to give up dancing. I'm crying with thankfulness."

That evening there was a celebration super with what were called toasts, but which were more often wishes, drunk by the grown-ups in wine provided by Gran and by the children in Coke.

"Let's each choose a toast," Alice suggested. "You start, Robin, because you are the youngest."

"Oh, I drink to Gemma and Sisters," said Robin. "Let there be lots and lots of performances next Christmas and tons of new songs swirled by me. And no more awful dancing matinee or school plays."

Philip looked at Lydia. "And now you."

150

Lydia raised her glass. "I know it's selfish, but I'm drinking a toast to me. I want you all to wish I'll be a very, very great dancer. I don't want anything else."

When they had drunk to Lydia, Alice turned to Gemma.

"What about you, darling? What's your toast?"

Gemma thought. "I think I'll drink to the new school. My wish is that I learn things there that will make me a great actress."

"Hoity-toity!" said Gran. "Great indeed! Don't forget pride comes before a fall."

To her surprise Ann found herself rushing to Gemma's defense. "Gemma's not conceited; she just knows she's good. You should have seen her as Lady Jane Grey."

Philip felt that was a subject best not pursued, for Gran did not want anyone except her grandchildren to shine, so he said quickly: "What's your toast, Ann?"

Ann looked puzzled. "I wish I knew. Sometimes I think it's to have the brains to go to a university, and then sometimes I think I'd like a scholarship to the Royal College of Music. More often I wish and wish we needn't grow up but could go on being like we are now forever and ever."

Alice smiled at Ann. "Your toast is rather like mine. I know you've all got to grow up and go your own ways, but there isn't a mom in the world who doesn't wish sometimes that her children would stay children for as long as possible."

"My toast is a wish really," said Philip. "I wish I could see into the future. I don't want you to grow up yet, I want us to live here as a family for as long as possible, but I'm terribly curious to know what happens to you all."

Gran held up her wineglass. "As the last to give a toast I know what mine must be. It's to the family, and that includes you, Gemma. Like you, Philip, I can't wait to know what happens next. I've a feeling exciting things may be waiting around the corner."